4 Jan 17

Te

Mi

K

Charles G. P. Kromes

What Did Eye See?

Charles G. P. Kramer

authorHOUSE

AuthorHouse™ UK
1663 Liberty Drive
Bloomington, IN 47403 USA
www.authorhouse.co.uk
Phone: 0800.197.4150

Published by AuthorHouse 08/18/2016

ISBN: 978-1-5246-6259-2 (sc)
ISBN: 978-1-5246-6260-8 (hc)
ISBN: 978-1-5246-6261-5 (e)

Foreword

Many years ago, I wrote an autobiography to let my three children know why I was frequently telling them off. In reality, a parent is only a page ahead in the book of life, and I wanted them to know where I went wrong as a youngster. I hoped that they wouldn't endanger themselves and make the same mistakes. As it turned out, it was an exercise in futility. The book has been enjoyed by many, resulting in my being encouraged to write my first novel.

The novel began as a trilogy, but after having written several thousands of words in each of the books, my son completely trashed the computer, and I lost the lot apart from about six thousand words that I had printed off on an old dot matrix printer. That was twenty-odd years ago, and it took several years before I again put pen to paper. This is the second novel that has an affiliation with the first, and it attempts to complete the story of some of the characters. I now save all my work on practically every medium available.

Acknowledgements

To my sister from different parents, Jane in Nanaimo, British Columbia, who assisted me with my first novel and who has proven to be an inspiration. She has encouraged me to improve my style, such as it is.

Also to my mentor, Chris Elmes, authoress of *The Overcoming*, and to my good friend Tina. They both very kindly read the book for content and enjoyment. Without the input of all three, this book would never have been published.

To Daniel Styler, who did the artwork for the front and back covers.

Other Publications by the Author

Errs and Places: A Humorous and Graphic Autobiography
Dawn and the Knight – A Reluctant Soldier

Children's Books

Douglas and the Ogly Flies
Douglas and the Barn in the Magic Forest
Did You Ever Wonder What Goes on in a Stone?

Dedicated to my dearest wife of almost forty-four years, and to the wonderful family with whom we have both been blessed.

CHAPTER 1

GEORGE O'ROURKE WAS floating in a twilight world and in a state of total confusion. He was vaguely aware that people were near him because he could hear voices, but they sounded an entire world away. He occasionally thought he had opened his eyes, but he did not see anything. He fell back into a strange, dreamlike state. It was all very odd, which only added to his anxiety. He knew he had been in this weird fantasy for many hours, but he wanted desperately to understand what was going on. He felt more tired than he had ever felt before.

After another long period of total void, he felt himself becoming more aware, and he could hear the voice of his wife, Jayne, who seemed to be calling to him from some distance away. He slowly felt he was becoming more lucid, and he gradually eased himself up and looked around. He didn't recognise his surroundings; it was fairly dark and clammy, but the sound of Jayne's voice was unmistakable and seemed to be getting farther away.

'Jayne!' he shouted. 'I'm in here, but I can't see you. Where are you?'

She called again, but he wasn't able to understand a word she was saying. He rose to his feet and began stumbling towards where her voice was coming from.

He was aware that he was in some kind of cave or a tunnel, but there didn't appear to be any sides. He kept looking around and listening intently for Jayne's voice, but it seemed as far away as ever. Eventually, he caught a glimpse of a twinkle of light, and so he ventured clumsily towards it. As he got closer, he could see what appeared to be an entrance, and so he continued to stagger towards it until eventually he came to an opening out on a long, sandy beach.

He looked around, but it was all very bewildering because closer inspection showed it wasn't a beach, and neither was it a desert. He had never seen anything like it before. He wandered around for a while, all the time calling out after Jayne, but she didn't reply. He then thought she must still be inside the cave, and so he ventured back in the direction of the entrance – but he couldn't find it. He began to panic and ran back and forth along from where he had exited, but the opening eluded him. The sun was now very bright, so much so that he had never known it to glow so intensely, yet it didn't seem hot enough considering its brilliance.

He looked along the sand dunes again, first to his left and then to his right. 'Jayne, it's me. Are you out here?'

He then heard a different voice, and for some reason he began to feel unwell. His breathing became more laboured, and he realised that he was in a great deal of pain.

As he looked in front of him to try to find the entrance yet again, he saw something small coming towards him at speed, and it hit him squarely in the chest. His whole body arched with the pain. Just as he was recovering, a second object hit him in exactly the same place. He was aware that he was losing consciousness, and the last thing he heard were voices that had an urgency about them. He then slid into oblivion.

He had no idea how long he had been unconscious, but finally he began to stir. His head ached really badly, and he had a raging thirst. In the background was an irritating noise that he couldn't identify, and there seemed to be a lot of activity around him. There was something in his hand that felt warm and comforting, and it seemed to be caressing him from his wrist down to the fingers. He struggled to open his eyes, and though it felt as if they were glued together, eventually he managed to force one open.

'Doctor, Doctor – his eyes are opening. He is coming to! Thank God!'

There was heightened activity around him, and he was aware that Jayne was sitting next to him and holding his hand as he gradually but slowly woke up. He was very muddled because he was in a bed, and he had no idea how he'd got there. He tried to form words into questions, but Jayne stopped him.

'Try not to speak, George. You have had a little accident, so just take your time.'

He was aware that there were other people in the room, and he heard a man's voice say, 'Well, I have to say, Mrs O'Rourke, for a moment I thought we were going to lose him. He's a tough old bird, I'll give him that. When his heart stopped a second time, and considering the mess he's in, I was about to call it. He is a very lucky man!'

Initially George thought that whoever it was who'd said that was referring to someone else, but when Jayne's soothing voice kept reassuring him that he was going to be all right, he realised that all the fuss was to do with him. He gradually became a little more articulate, but he still found it a struggle to form any words. Jayne's comforting presence reassured him, and so he fell into a light sleep and relaxed.

It was some time later when he again became aware of his surroundings. Still at his side was Jayne, his wife of three years. They had met at a military convention over three years earlier; Jayne was a military police sergeant, and George had just been demobbed from the SAS. They were married in Alverstoke Church in Gosport, but they had to delay their honeymoon until George had finally left the service.

Having rested reasonably well, he was better able to talk and understand what was being said to him. 'Where am I, and what happened, Jayne?' he asked. 'How did I get here, and who put me in bed?'

'You have been in an accident, George. A car ran you over, but you are going to be all right now. Just rest and get your strength back! You have been comatose for five days, and you have scared the living bejabbers out of me. Now, rest. I'm not going anywhere.'

George had to stay in the hospital for another two weeks before the doctors felt he was well enough to be allowed home. Once there and surrounded with all his home comforts, he tried to remember what had happened, but it was a complete blank.

'Has anyone been arrested for running me over?' he asked.

Jayne replied that it had been a hit and run, but the police were trying to trace an R Reg Volkswagen Golf. 'Apparently it was a vivid green, so it shouldn't too difficult to trace.'

George thought about it for a while but felt that after three weeks, it was most unlikely they would ever find it.

The following morning, a police constable came to ask George some questions about the accident. George racked his brains, but all he could remember was running along Stokes Bay as he did every morning, and then nothing – his mind was a complete blank.

'It would appear that it was deliberate, Mr O'Rourke. Do you know if you have any enemies?'

'Deliberate? How do you know, and why would anyone want to do that?'

'We have witnesses who saw the car, and it seemed to be waiting because as you ran past it, the occupant started the engine and deliberately ran into you. It happened so quickly that the witnesses were unable to get the full registration, but they have given a good description of the vehicle. Have you been out running regularly at the same time each day, using the same route?'

George nodded and explained that he liked to keep his body trim because after having left the armed forces recently, he didn't want to turn to flab.

George had in fact been in the Special Forces but had been wounded in the left shoulder. The surgeons had done a magnificent job in rebuilding the bones, but it had left him with a slight limitation of movement which, he was warned, would never be 100 per cent again. As a result, George was offered a desk job but decided enough was enough; he would start a new career.

The constable ventured that whoever the culprit was, it was clear that George's movements had been monitored very closely in order to launch this attempt on his life. 'Your wife tells me that you were in the Special Forces. Is there any chance that one of your deployments could have caused animosity towards you?'

George was a little perturbed that Jayne had volunteered the information about his past to the constable, because it was something that was never talked about outside the confines of the regiment. Casting aside his misgivings, he replied, 'Most likely there are dozens of, shall we say, unhappy people. But they were from a specific part of the world, and I would have been dressed as a local, so it is very unlikely for anyone to have any idea where I live.'

'I think you need to be very careful from now on. Check everything, and don't have any regular routines. As much as we'd like to, we don't have the manpower to watch you twenty-four seven, but we will be redoubling our efforts to find the culprit.'

Chapter 2

GEORGE AND JAYNE had only been dating for a few months before George had popped the question. They both had a great deal in common: both were fitness fanatics and were experts in unarmed combat. Jayne was also a black belt second Dan in Shotokan Karate, and George was a third Dan. They had small circles of friends, most of whom were either still in the armed forces or had just left.

They decided that once George was ensconced in civilian life as a PE teacher, they would start a family. Jayne had only just left the army in the previous week and was undecided about a career in civilian life. His best man, nicknamed Murky, was still in the Special Air Service. Murky had earned his nickname because of the way he'd worked whilst on operations. He had the ability to infiltrate and move freely amongst the most unsavoury people.

They honeymooned in Greece and then decided that George would begin his teacher training on their return. He already had his degree in languages, which was to be the second subject in his teaching career. For her part, Jayne felt she would also like to be involved in schools, but not in the same one as George because they believed it would impact their private lives too much. In fact, they both behaved quite differently when in a working environment.

George performed well in his interview and was offered a position at Bay House School. This was very convenient for him because it meant that he could run along Stokes Bay and head into the school, where there were shower facilities, enabling him to get ready for the day ahead.

Once George was back home, Jayne, who had finally decided to become temporarily employed in a school to keep herself gainfully employed, had been given two weeks' leave to aid in his convalescence. She intended to seek employment with the police once they had settled down with a family.

They both talked a great deal about what had happened, but the more they thought about it, the less sense it made.

George cast his mind back over the months since his demob to try to think of any potential enemies that he might have made, but he and Jayne had blended into their surroundings without any fuss at all.

They had bought a house in Fieldmore Road from a couple whom George knew very well, both were teachers at Baycroft School and had lived there for twenty-three years. Their children, James and Samantha, had grown up and were now at university, and Danny and Dawn Knight had decided to downsize to a smaller house.

George's connection with Danny and Dawn began several years earlier when Danny and his friend Stuart threw an egg over the back wall, making a mess of the kitchen window. They were both marched around through the front door and into the back garden, and they were made to clear up the mess. George really liked the house then and knew that one day, he would make it his own. He didn't know how, but he knew that without doubt, it would be his.

Their relationship grew further when, a couple of years later, he and Stuart had been kidnapped by an arms smuggling gang and whisked off to Africa. It was only by pure chance that just as they were about to be murdered, they ran into a group of mercenaries led by Hendrik Van Hove and Danny, who had left the paras to become a mercenary.

It was this adventure, and the way in which Danny was so highly trained in unarmed combat that encouraged George to join the army and move on to Special Forces.

For his part, Stuart had married George's sister Katy and had confounded his parents by making a career on the stage as a comedian. Stuart was a superb motor mechanic, and his father had hoped that he would take over the family business, but the publicity Stuart had received at the press conference on their return home had given him a huge advantage. They were both currently in a double act, touring America, and the American public couldn't get enough of them.

Since Danny had been in the paras and was also a mercenary for a number of years, George contacted him to ask if he knew of any possible enemies he might have made. There was the slim chance that because he now owned the house, it could be a case of mistaken identity. Danny ventured the opinion that since so many years had passed, if anyone had wanted him dispensed with, it would have happened before now. George also suggested this theory to the police, who considered the possibility. They looked at records of recently released long-term prisoners who might have had some form of contact with Danny, but that drew a blank and only added to the confusion.

Eventually, Jayne asked George if he thought it possible that someone he knew in the armed forces might be gunning for him. He gave it a great deal of thought, but he knew deep down that the people in his unit were loyal, trustworthy, and like family. 'No, poppet. I have racked my brains and can think of no reason who would want me badly injured or dead.'

The following weeks kept them both on their toes and alert. George changed his daily routine, and Jayne took a different route whenever she went out. It was a precaution in case whoever had it in for George might use her to get at him.

It was a difficult time for them both, and trying to remain alert every day was tiring in the extreme. There were lapses in concentration from time to time, but thankfully they went without incident. After a while, George began to think that the police might have been mistaken, because time was passing without any further occurrences. He thought if it was a genuine attempt on his life, another attempt would have been made by now.

This situation went on for about six months. Eventually George became suspicious that he was being observed and sometimes followed. At first he thought he was imagining it, but there were faces in the crowd that became a little too familiar. Since the first attempt on his life had been a hit and run, he thought that any future attempt would be similar, but now he wasn't so sure. As a result, he made sure he would be more careful, and he often stopped to either check a shop window or tie a lace while furtively looking around for anything suspicious.

Again, this became tedious and very difficult to keep up for long periods of time. George began to wish that someone would make a move, simply so that he could deal with it because constantly being on one's guard was unsustainable.

He was trying to remain alert to anything unusual, and although there had been instances where he had felt uncomfortable about specific occurrences, they usually amounted to nothing.

Every now and then, he would become suspicious of anyone appearing to follow him, but once it appeared the perceived threat was just someone going about their business, he relaxed again. It was inevitable that he would relax more and continue with his routine, albeit a disruptive one.

This went on for several weeks, when he started to get a bad feeling, and the hairs on the back of his neck began prickle. He knew he was being watched but never managed to see anyone or anything.

The worrying thing was seeing the side gate of the house open occasionally, and he wasn't sure whether or not it was the window cleaners. They would sometimes leave a chit to say they had called, but not always.

He was highly suspicious that someone was playing cat and mouse with him, obviously trying to wear him down. It was more than likely that they knew what he was capable of because of his background, and therefore he would be more on his guard.

The situation was very wearing and started to grate on his nerves. He was clearly worried for Jayne in case she also became a target with whomever it was stalking him. It was possible that they may believe she had been told of what they felt George had seen.

Finally, it happened. His stalkers made their move when they clearly felt George had been worn down enough for him to be off guard. It was one evening when he left school slightly later than usual. He'd had a particularly trying day at work with some disruptive pupils, and owing to a lapse of concentration, he hadn't noticed he was being followed by two men. It started quite innocently with him walking down Vectis Road. He had heard a car slowly pull up behind him and stopping with doors slamming shut. He looked behind and observed two people but thought nothing more about it because they looked harmless enough. Suddenly and without warning, they had both closed in on George, bundling him into a garden with one of his assailants trying to pass a cord over his head.

His mind was instantly focused, and his training kicked in. He rolled with the momentum of his assailants as they tried to control his movement, which took them by surprise. He instinctively put his hands between the cord and pushed upwards, making an apex with his arms. He then prised the cord apart and managed to roll away, jumping immediately to his feet. One of the men had recovered more quickly than the other, and as he began his attack, George kicked him squarely in the groin; the man went down like a sack of potatoes, screaming in agony. Before George was able to get in position to tackle the second man, the assailant had made a dash back out to the road, where a car rushed up, stopped rapidly, and picked him up. He wasn't able to get the number because it happened too quickly.

Just then, the front door opened because of all the noise, and an elderly gentleman shouted out that he had called the police. Thinking fast, George went to his victim, used all his strength, gathered him up, and made his apologies to the house's occupant. He said that it was just a stilly prank that went very wrong, and the police would not be necessary. He begged the man to cancel the call.

'The police are far too busy to deal with high jinks, sir, and I *am* sorry we fell in your garden,' said George.

The gentleman replied that he hadn't really called them; he'd only said it to scare them off. He said because it was a joke, he was happy to let it go. Looking at the man George was holding, the old man asked if he was all right and whether he needed any help. George replied that he was merely winded and would be fine. Satisfied, the person went back into his house, leaving George and his attacker to their own devices.

What the occupant didn't see was George's hand securely clasped over the mouth of the other person, who was still trying to recover from the well-aimed kick.

George dragged him out of the garden struggling. George was a fairly big and powerful man, and he managed to get the man to a quieter area. There he began to question him. A passer-by looked out of curiosity, and George kept saying, 'Are you all right? You've had a nasty fall.'

All this time, he was obscuring his victim from view, with his powerful hands around his throat. Once the coast was clear he said, 'You've got two minutes to tell me what's going on before I really hurt you!'

The man looked up at George and spat in his face. 'Go stuff yourself – like my friend is seeing to your wife right now!'

George wrenched the man's neck, breaking it instantly. After dumping the body in the garden, he hurriedly left the scene. He didn't know or care if the passer-by would be able to identify him when the body was found, because his main priority now was to get home to Jayne. He ran as fast as he could to get there to make sure she was safe.

It seemed to take an age before he finally arrived, but as he approached, the house was in complete darkness. He was terrified, not knowing what to expect inside, but he knew he had to go in.

He used the darkest area by the wall to try to conceal himself as he made his way around the back. Keeping a low profile, he climbed the wall and rolled over the top, landing lightly on his feet.

He remained crouched, and all his senses worked in overdrive as he carefully assessed the garden and looked into the house for any sign of movement. He cursed the street lamp that illuminated a great deal of the garden, and he gingerly skirted the wall and made his way towards the kitchen. It was with some trepidation that he noticed the door was partially open. Feeling he had surprise on his side, he rushed in to confront whoever might be there.

As he ran in, he encountered a person in his way who had managed to sidestep his rush forward, and he found himself on his back with a foot across his neck. He was about to react when he heard Jayne's voice saying, 'Losing your touch, O'Rourke?'

Looking up, he saw her smiling at him, and his relief was overwhelming. Once he had composed himself, he asked if he was allowed up, and she removed her foot from him. He stood. 'I am assuming something has gone down here, because this is not normal behaviour. What's happened?'

Jayne explained the knock at the door. Although she opened it with caution, it was forcibly pushed inwards, taking her by surprise. 'At first I thought it was you horsing around, but when I realised it wasn't, I became a little frightened. He was a big man but was not very agile; he relied heavily on his bulk.'

George listened and asked what happened next.

'As he came at me, I adopted a defensive stance. There wasn't room to manoeuvre, so I allowed him to come close. When the time was right, I thrust my forefinger into his left eye. It went right in, and it was disgusting.' With that, she broke down; it was fear and adrenaline that had kept her composed, but now that she was safe with George, she was unable to hold it all in.

'I thought they had killed you, George, and I didn't know what to do. When I saw you come over the wall the way you hid in the shadows, I thought it was one of them, until you began to make your way towards the house. You were walking like a monkey.'

With the release of fear and a mixture of relief and pent-up anxiety, they both fell about laughing.

'Where is he now, then?' George asked.

'He is still in the lounge, where he fell.'

'Okay, we need to think what we are going to do now. It won't be long before the body of my would-be assailant is discovered, and we don't have time to move this one.'

Jayne was naturally anxious to know whether he was seen by the house owner or the passer-by and George explained that he felt he was easily recognisable because he was a big man, and his face had been partially lit by the street lamp.

'Pack a couple of bags, Jayne. We have to go into hiding.'

'Won't it be better if we ring the police now and let them deal with it?'

George explained that to try to pass off one dead body to them would be difficult enough, but two might cause them to be kept under house arrest. This would put them both at greater risk. 'The thing is, poppet, the police are busy enough as it is. Without anything tangible to go on, they will need us both handy in order to establish facts as they become apparent. It would leave us exposed to any further attacks, and next time we might not be so lucky! There is also the possibility that we won't be believed, and that would draw unwelcome attention.'

They drove to the nearest cashpoint, taking all their individual credit and debit cards, and they drew out the maximum amount possible. With the cash they already had, they accrued over fifteen hundred pounds.

Then they went home, opened up the Internet, and booked their car on to the first sailing of the Isle of Wight ferry to Fishbourne the next morning. They booked return tickets in order to not raise any unwelcome questions, although they had no intention of coming back the same way. George hadn't quite thought his plan through yet, but he had a good idea of what he was going to do.

'If we are lucky, the police won't be informed about the body I dumped in someone's front garden until tomorrow morning. Even then, they may not connect that person to me until the end of the day, which should give us time to get away. If we don't get on that ferry for whatever reason, it has been a blast being with you. It is possible we won't make it. We have to leave now, and just in case, we won't book in to an hotel; we'll have an uncomfortable night in the car instead. That way we can park up in a car park and generally keep out of the way.'

Jayne agreed with George's reasoning, and so they went in to the local ASDA to buy provisions to see them through the night.

They drove to a car park in Hardway, and once they felt they were reasonably obscure, they tried to fathom what on earth was going on.

'Do you think you may have suffered minor amnesia, George, and you may have forgotten something crucial?' Jayne suggested.

George thought about it for a minute and started recounting memories from a period well before the attempts on his life had started. He began just before he had left the army with Jayne, prompting him on some of the greyer areas. Although they still drew a blank, it wasn't a waste of time, because it did occupy them though the long night.

At four the following morning, George nudged Jayne, who had just started to doze, to say it was time to go. 'We are booked on the five fifteen sailing, darling. Let's hope no one has raised the alarm. The first body they find will be the one I left in that front garden, and if I had been recognised, they will find the second body at our house. Let's hope the owner of the house in question is a late riser!'

They approached the ferry terminal and were ushered to a lane, where George got out of the car to collect the ticket. His heart was in his throat as he approached the building, fearing that he would be accosted, but the whole operation went smoothly, and he returned to the car with some very welcome hot drinks for them both.

The line to get on was one of the longest waits imaginable, but within a few minutes, the queues were beginning to move forward. Just as George was about to embark, the usher stopped the car. He wasn't sure whether they should get out and make a break for it, but when he realised that it was only to let another queue start, he relaxed again. After a few more minutes, they were again called forward, and finally they gave a huge sigh of relief as they drove up to their allotted space, where they locked up and walked up the stairs to join the other passengers.

The journey took about forty-five minutes when an announcement was made for all passengers to return to their vehicles. The engines were started, but within a few minutes, there were several car horns sounding off until a further announcement was made, asking Mr and Mrs O'Rourke to return to their vehicle. This was repeated several times, and when no one responded, the crew feared the worst. Once all the vehicles had disembarked, a complete search of the ferry was conducted; revealing that the couple had either fallen overboard or had completely disappeared.

The helicopter from Daedalus was scrambled to conduct a search pattern around the Solent using heat-sensing cameras, and a number of small craft joined in. By dusk, it was deemed to be futile. A further attempt was made the following morning, but again there was no sign of the O'Rourke's.

CHAPTER 3

'I THOUGHT YOU said that you only killed two people between you!' Murky said.

'What do you mean?' Jayne asked. 'Is there another body somewhere, then?'

Murky went on to explain that there had been three murders in Gosport, and both Jayne and George were wanted by the police in order to eliminate them from their enquiries.

George and Jayne were naturally curious about his question and so requested to see the newspaper.

Murky replied, 'Well, it seems they no longer think we were both drowned in the Solent, then. It hasn't taken them long to figure it out, but I guess with cameras everywhere on board, they would have seen you drive on alone with your van and drive off with two passengers.'

Jayne said she was surprised that it only took a couple of weeks, because she and George had taken spare clothes with them when they left home. When they got changed in the washrooms, Jayne had put on a ginger wig. They would have looked completely different when they got into Murky's van.

'Actually, darling, the police aren't stupid; all they had to do was go over footage of the recordings, and they would have clocked pretty much all of our movements throughout the journey.'

Murky told George to look further down the page, where the reporter added that the police also wanted to speak to a certain David Murphy, also known as Murky, in connection with the O'Rourke's and their apparent disappearance.

Murky had contacted his commanding officer and explained.

'The old man has told me to take the four weeks' leave I am due, and he said he knows nothing about where I intend to spend the time. We have got about a month to solve this thing, George, but beyond that, you are on your own.'

Jayne was concerned that once the four weeks were up, Murky might have difficulty explaining his involvement with them, and also why he hadn't come forward when the news bulletin went out.

Murky said, 'It won't be difficult to explain it away. Yes, I helped you out, but I had no idea why until I returned to barracks from leave. Since some of my leaves tend to be on survival-type jollies, I rarely take a radio with me, so I wouldn't have been aware of anything untoward.'

There was silence for a few moments, and then George suddenly realised the significance of what Murky had said. 'Three bodies? You did say three bodies?'

George reached for the paper again and read it again. It suddenly dawned on them that up until now, they had had no lead whatsoever. The third body might give them an idea of what it had all been about, because there had to be a link somewhere.

'It says here that the first body was found in a shallow grave inside Anne's Hill Cemetery, and it is reminding the public that the story had broken some seven months earlier.'

The article went on to say that as reported in the press at the time, the victim had been shot and had had his hands tied behind his back. The police were not sure at the moment of how all three deaths were connected, because the other two bodies that were recently found had been killed differently from the one in Anne's Hill.

There was also a photo of George and Jayne's neighbours, who were said to have been shocked on finding out that someone had been killed next door. 'They seemed like such a nice, quiet couple,' they'd said.

The story went on to explain that George was a friend and brother-in-law to Stuart Baxter, who was now on tour in the United States. The public were reminded that both boys had been kidnapped by an arms smuggling gang and whisked off to Africa.

George mumbled, 'Bloody hell, don't they just love to dig up the past? Anything to enhance a story.'

'This other murder has to be connected to why someone wants me out of the way.' George racked his brains trying to think back three months, to the time when this was

23

supposed to have happened. 'The only thing I can think of is that I sometimes run through the cemetery because I enjoy the tranquillity within the grounds.'

'Well, buddy, you need to think really hard, and quickly, because something clearly went down while you were in there, and somebody must have seen you!'

George was silent for a while before he suddenly remembered something. 'Hang on a minute. I seem to recall some activity on the opposite side of the grounds, when I had slowed down to a walk. I didn't really pay any attention to it, but on thinking back, it was a bit strange.'

Jayne asked what he meant by strange.

'It's just that I noticed there were a few people well away from the rows of new burials, under some trees and near the boundary wall. I thought they might be gardening or something, but it was almost dusk, and on reflection, they weren't really dressed for that kind of thing.'

Murky felt they were getting somewhere now and prompted George to think harder. 'Were there any signs of someone struggling or looking a little distressed? Where there any vehicles in the grounds or just outside as you entered or left? Come on, George. Concentrate.'

George thought a bit more. There were no signs of a struggle, but he did remember there being a black Daimler Jaguar parked at the entrance on Anne's Hill Road.

'Well, since we have nothing else to go on, let's start there,' Jayne said.

'Murky, doesn't your brother work in Scotland Yard?'

Murky knew where this was leading and reminded them that he too was wanted for questioning regarding the matter. 'If I contact my brother and declare myself interested, it would mean I am not where I say I am, effectively blowing our story out of the water. It is likely that he will have already been asked some awkward questions as to my whereabouts. If he is under some sort of scrutiny, he won't be able to help. But that aside, can you think back, George? This is all we have to go on. Did you happen to get any of the registration?'

'Not really. It wasn't a brand-new one, but it was really well looked after. I think it was a Y Reg 2000 model, making it four years old. I remember looking at it because I have always wanted one for myself, but I didn't really pay enough attention to the rest of the registration number.'

They sat and pondered for a while until Jayne suggested they eat something; they might think more clearly on a full stomach.

After deliberating and looking at all the possibilities, they still drew a blank. Finally, they decided to brainstorm their possible options, looking at ways they could trace the car without exposing their position.

Jayne produced a sheet of paper and said, 'Right. The first column is the idea, the second is the benefit, and the third is the likely outcome.'

Going online was ruled out because they could be traced, and the same was true with mobile phones. Eventually, Murky said that there was really only one option left to them. 'I need to break cover and leave you on your own so that once suspicion has been lifted from me; I can feed you information surreptitiously as and when I find it.

George and Jayne were naturally curious as to how he was going to explain why, when they had contacted him, they had asked him to take them off the ferry in his van in order to give the impression they had drowned.

'I will tell the police that you had told me about another attempt on your lives, and that you needed to disappear. I will say that you didn't elaborate about killing anyone, and so as soon as I found out that I was also needed for questioning, I decided to come in and explain all I knew. The police will more than likely buy it because they are clearly not resourced to keep a watchful eye. They will no doubt want to question me about where I last saw you, and they will know we got straight on the Red Funnel Ferry to Southampton.'

They had in fact driven from Southampton to Bristol, where Murky had the keys to a friend's flat. His friend worked at MoD Abbey Wood and used it as a stopover during the week.

Murky went on to explain that because this was only a temporary base, it was time they disappeared properly in order that stayed well hidden.

George said, 'Your friend doesn't know we are here, does he?'

Murky nodded affirmatively and said that he was going to arrange to smuggle them to France, to a little village called Étaples. 'There is an old comrade of my fathers who retired there several years ago with his wife. They will be only too pleased to shelter you until we get to the bottom of this.' He went on to say that they only had a few days before his friend returned from leave, and he would naturally want his flat back.

Murky's plan was to get George and Jayne back down to the south coast, where he would organise another friend who had a fairly large yacht to smuggle them over.

They were concerned about how this could happen when all three of them were wanted by the police. Murky reassured them that he had his ways, and he told them it would be achieved with the aid of some associates that they didn't actually know.

The following morning, Murky told the O'Rourke's that he was popping out for some groceries, and they should both stay in the flat. 'We don't want anyone seeing you, and believe me; I can mingle in with the locals without them knowing I am there.'

George and Jayne busied themselves around the flat while he was out, but they became more worried as the hours ticked by with no sign of him. It crossed their minds that he may have been apprehended, and they began to plan how they were going to get back to Gosport.

George said, 'Murky would never disclose our whereabouts to the police, but if he has been arrested, they will know that we are likely to be in the area as well.'

They decided that they would wait until after dark to move out; first, it would give Murky more time, and second, they could prepare for the long haul southwards.

Just after lunch, the phone started to ring, which made them both jump. They decided not to answer it just in case it was the tenant, who would ask too many questions about who they were. It rang off, and then a few moments later, it started to ring again.

'It could be Murky, but I am not taking the risk. One wrong move now could find us in real trouble.'

They were both sitting in silence, pondering what could have happened, and suddenly they heard a key being inserted in the door.

Not given easily over to panic, they quietly got off of the sofa and made their way to the bathroom. There, they waited to see who it was. If it was the tenant, they would try to reason with him. If that failed, they decided that they would tie him up in a locked room and ring the police once they were well clear of the area.

They were holding their breath as the door opened, and they listened to the footsteps as the person moved about the room. The movement appeared to be measured and deliberate, giving the impression that the person was suspicious of their presence.

As the footsteps got nearer to their position, they prepared to pounce on the unsuspecting intruder when Murky called out their names.

With a huge sigh of relief, they left the bathroom and joined Murky in the lounge. 'We were beginning to get worried when you didn't show up, and we started to make contingency plans to get us out of here,' George said.

'Yes, I'm sorry about that, but I did try to ring you a few times to reassure you all was well. The problem I have had is that the old girl has finally given up the ghost – cam belt, I'm afraid. I went around the back streets to find an old garage and bought another old banger of a van that should last me for a couple of years. The proprietor was brilliant; he didn't ask any questions, went out to tow the old girl back to his yard, and sold me the one I have now.'

'Isn't it time you got yourself a decent car old, mate?'

'I already have one, George. It is a two-year-old Citroen C5. It's a lovely car, but I use old bangers as run-arounds. Anyway, I have managed to contact my friend, and it is on for him to get you both to France.'

The following day, the whole journey was organised, and within a short time they were heading away from Bristol. Finally they arrived on the A34 and headed towards Gosport. From there, Murky told them both he was taking them to Hardway.

'As you obviously know, George, there is a hard standing by the Hardway Sailing Club where we can park. The yacht will be waiting to whisk you both off to pastures new and get the pair of you out of the way for a while.'

The traffic was fairly heavy but still moving at a reasonable pace. Some cars were being driven really aggressively, and once a gap appeared, someone would push in. After a while, the traffic ahead opened up considerably. Murky put his foot down to gained speed when a car in the fast lane pulled across his front, cutting him up and causing him to brake hard.

'Hold tight, guys. This could be nasty.'

The words were barely out of Murky's mouth when they had to break suddenly, which ended in a huge collision in the back of their car.

'Oh, hell! That's torn it!' George exclaimed in horror. 'If the police attend this, we could be in trouble.'

Once they had composed themselves, Murky looked back and saw that the occupants in the car behind had clearly suffered badly; the passenger in the rear seat couldn't have been properly belted in. Both airbags had operated, but there was a head between the two front passengers against a cracked windscreen, accompanied by copious amounts of blood.

Thinking quickly, the three of them made a hurried plan and waited for the inevitable crowd of good Samaritans and ghouls who would get out of their cars to help or watch on with morbid curiosity.

'Right, gently get out of the car and mingle with the people who are attempting to help. See if you can quietly secrete yourself over the bank and get to the nearest road to catch a lift. The yacht is called the *Queen Charlotte,* and the skipper is an old mate of mine called Josh. He will land you in France. He has drawn two thousand euros on the strength that I will pay him back, so you both owe me. Now, for goodness' sake, keep a low profile and try to get to the yacht as quickly as you can. As for the police, as far as they are concerned, I was driving home to get in touch regarding my helping you the other week. Good luck, guys.

I will talk to my brother Ethan once the heat is off me, and I'll get in touch when I can.'

They gave their thanks, left the car, and joined the crowd, pretending to be concerned with helping. While all the attention of the crowd was on trying to help the passengers, George took advantage of the confusion and climbed the bank first. Once he found a suitable bush to conceal himself, he whistled to Jayne, who then joined him. They looked back from their cover to see if there was anyone watching them, but they had managed to slip away unnoticed.

They realised that if they were seen approaching a road from the undergrowth, it would look suspicious, so they adopted escape-and-evasion tactics, keeping out of sight until they were safely on the road. They tried to thumb a lift, and several cars passed them by until eventually an elderly couple stopped and asked where they were going.

George replied, 'Hello, this is my wife, Jenny, and we have been on a hitch-hiking holiday. My name is Stuart, and we are making our way home to Bridgemary in Gosport.'

The old boy looked at them suspiciously, saying, 'Travelling light for a hiking holiday, aren't you?'

'We have had to cut it short because when we went shopping in the nearest village, our tent was stolen, along with a few things we'd left at the site. The two guys who had pitched up next to us seemed to be decent blokes, but they were obviously not as nice as we thought.'

'Okay, then. Hop in. We can take you as far as Fareham – not far to go after that.

There were a few moments of silence when the man began showing an interest in where they had been and what they did for a living. Cleary George couldn't say he was a teacher, because it was term time, but Jayne said she worked for the Hampshire police. This seemed to satisfy him, but the wife began to whisper in her husband's ear.

Suddenly, he pulled in. 'I thought I had seen you two before. You are all over the papers and television. You are both murderers. Get out!'

With that, Jayne pulled out her lipstick, thrust it in the wife's neck, and said menacingly, 'I have a small gun pointed at your wife, and if you don't keep driving, I will pull the trigger!'

This took them both by surprise, and they were clearly shaken. 'Listen, we are too old to do you any harm. If you let us go, we promise we won't raise the alarm at all. We promise, don't we, Dorothy?'

Poor Dorothy was shaking wildly and was clearly scared.

'Sorry, but we really can't afford to take that risk. Please pull out and take us to Bridgemary. I promise, neither of you will be harmed.

The man did as he was told and began driving again. His wife was sobbing now and they both felt really sorry for her.

'Now, listen to me, both of you,' George said reassuringly. 'You both know what we are capable of, but please allow us to tell you what has really happened. Then we hope you will understand why we are on the run. Please, Dorothy, don't be upset.'

With that, Jayne put the lipstick tube away and told her it was alright. 'I wouldn't dream of hurting you Dorothy but we are really desperate.'

This calmed down Dorothy, and so they told them what had happened. They explained that they had in fact killed two men between them because they were defending themselves, but the third one was a mystery.

George explained, 'I think I may have witnessed something to do with that murder, but at the moment, I can't think what it is all about. I don't know how much the press have elaborated and embellished the story, but Jayne and I used our bare hands to defend ourselves, and the other man died by being shot in the back of the head. We don't possess any weapons, and we give an absolute promise it was neither of us.'

Dorothy said that she knew the man had been shot in the head and that the police had stated it was different than the other two murders.

George and Jayne went on to tell them about the attack with the car, and how the police seemed powerless to protect them.

There was a short silence, and Dorothy's husband said, 'My name is Robert Jenkins, and this is my wife, Dotty. Call me an old fool, but I believe you.'

'Thank you so much, Robert. It does mean a great deal to us, and we hope you will give us time to get away before you raise the alarm.'

Robert said that he didn't intend to, but George told him that he must so that they were not held responsible for aiding and abetting.

'You're not really going to Bridgemary, are you, son?' Robert said. 'Tell us where you are really headed, and we'll take you there. That will be all right, won't it, Dotty?'

Having listened to their story, Dorothy seemed much more relaxed and believed their sincerity. She looked at both of them and said that she was sorry she and her husband had panicked. They would tell the police they had in fact stopped to pick them up. 'We won't tell anybody where we drop you off exactly, but we'll tell them we last saw you in Bridgemary. Will that be all right, my dears?'

Jayne, now feeling relieved, squeezed Dorothy's hand tightly but gently, letting her know how grateful she was.

George tapped Jayne's leg, and when she looked at him, he gave her a look, letting her know not to say anything.

'We are getting in a small boat to go back to the Isle of Wight. The police won't suspect that we would have returned because the search there had drawn a blank. If you could kindly take us to the Gosport ferry and drop us off at the Castle Tavern, we would be more grateful than you will ever know. We have a friend in there waiting to take us over in his launch.'

They still had some way to go, and so the conversation turned away from their current circumstances. Robert wanted to know more about George's encounter with the arms smuggling gang years before, and the subsequent kidnapping with his friend Stuart.

'We have seen Stuart perform. He is so funny, isn't he, Dotty?' They both began reiterating some of the things they'd heard him say, and they laughed at the memory of his show. Stuart had been recognised as having a natural talent and was effectively noticed at the press conference he gave on their being rescued. Naturally, their experiences had given him a great deal of raw material.

George said that they were still the very best of friends and had kept in contact all these years. Also, Stuart had married George's sister Katy.

It was a very relaxed drive to Gosport, and when they finally arrived at the Castle Tavern, Robert pulled over to let them out of the car. Dorothy got out, gave them both a big hug, and wished them luck in finding out the truth about what had happened.

'When shall we contact the police, George?' Robert asked.

'If you could pretend you dropped us off here at eleven o'clock tonight, but not tell them until first thing in the morning, that would be wonderful. But you must tell them where you let us out, just in case someone notices us getting out of your car. Just one thing, though: the police will find a flaw in your story because of the amount of time that has lapsed. They will push you for answers, but tell them we threatened to get you if you didn't lie for us, and because you knew we were murderers, you were very frightened. Okay?'

They both nodded, letting George know they understood.

'Thank you both once again for your kindness. We will never forget what you have done. Goodbye.'

The old couple both gave a warm smile and went into the car park to turn around. Then they drove off towards Fareham.

George and Jayne watched as they disappeared into the distance, and then they crossed the road to keep as much space from the drop-off point as possible.

'Why did you tell them this was where we wanted to be dropped off, and why the lie about going back on the island? Didn't you trust them?'

George said that with the best will in the world, once they had reported to the police, there was a chance they would inadvertently say something wrong, which the police would pick up on. It was far too risky letting them know everything.

It had been dark for about an hour when Robert and Dorothy had let them out of the car, and so they crossed the road to get to the Gosport High Street without anyone paying attention to them. The walk to Hardway wouldn't take long because George knew the area well; it was where he and Stuart had played together as youngsters, and it was also where Stuart's family still lived.

Once at the sailing club, they walked down to the hard and waited by one of the mooring bollards that an old tank landing craft used to be chained to. This was the prearranged meeting place, and they knew that they had to wait to be approached by Josh, who would ask if they had seen his little dog. It was an innocent enough question which would let them know they were talking to the right person. They sat on the log by the sailing club fence and waited for what seemed an eternity. George was getting a little worried and began to discuss a plan B with Jayne.

It was a clear night with wisps of cloud flitting across the skies. There was a light wind, causing them both to shiver; the only sound was the splashing of oars on water as someone was rowing a dinghy ashore. They both watched with interest as the occupant moored the little craft to the club pontoon and walked along until he reached the clubhouse, where he stopped and looked around. George decided to stand and glance in his direction to check if it might possibly be Josh. The man started to walk towards them and began to whistle, as if calling out to a dog. As the man approached George, he asked if he had seen his dog.

By this time Jayne was standing. Not wishing to take any chances, she shouted, 'Oh, my goodness. Long time, no see – at least, I think I know you. It's Josh, isn't it?'

Although dark, both George and Jayne saw a huge smile as the man replied. 'Ah, finally. I have had binoculars watching the bollard for the last few hours. I was beginning to worry you weren't going to make it! When I saw you sit there, I felt it had to be you.'

They both explained what had happened and about being picked up by the old couple.

Josh said, 'As it is, we have missed the tide tonight, because where I am moored, I am in a channel. The entrance has silted over, but we should be able to cast off any time after six in the morning.'

They walked along the pontoon and got into the dinghy, where Josh cast off and began to row out to his yacht. As they came alongside, they could see what a magnificent vessel the *Charlotte* was. Once they embarked, they marvelled at the interior.

Josh saw their faces and said there were three bedrooms and two wet rooms inside, as well as a very comfortable seating area.

Once they had both settled in, George realised how hungry he was; they hadn't eaten since breakfast. He said, 'It's been a tough day, Josh, and I have to say I'm starving and thirsty. Any chance of something to eat?'

Josh had some steak and kidney pies with a choice of tea, coffee, water, stout, or wine. 'Nothing hot, I'm afraid, because I didn't want to go shopping for fear of missing when you arrived. I had no idea what time you were due to get here. This will fill an empty space until we get under way tomorrow. I will nip to the supermarket before we slip the mooring and grab some eggs and bacon for breakfast, with some nice baps. A good, hearty meal should set you on your way for when you go ashore. I know a place I can take you to stay with some friends, but more about that later. Oh, and before I forget, here's the money Murky asked me to give you – two thousand euros. I have been drawing it out a bit at a time from different travel agents and the post office over the last three days. I didn't want any awkward questions about where was I going on the off chance someone might have paid any attention to me.'

'Thanks, Josh. We will repay Murky as soon as we can. By the way, how do you know him?'

'We were at school together. I know a lot about you two, but for some reason, we have never met. You know Murky – he doesn't socialise much.'

They sat and ate their meal, drinking copious amounts of tea. When they were satisfied, Josh suggested they get some sleep.

'I want to jump ashore just before the shops open in the morning, quickly drive to the nearest one, and buy breakfast.'

'Yes, Josh, so you said earlier. But having thought about it, would it be possible to forget breakfast, as good as it sounds? The thing is, the Jenkins' will be speaking to the police by that time, so it would probably be best if we set off as early as possible'.

'Okay, guys, but I have to say the weather looks like it is going to close in quite a bit from dawn onwards. It's going to be a bit of a choppy one, I'm afraid.'

George asked whether Josh was happy about the undertaking given that a storm was brewing, but Josh reassured them that it was likely to be a wind strength of force five. 'It will be a bit uncomfortable, but nothing too serious.' He went on to explain that he had sailed in some of the worst storms imaginable around the Baltic Sea.

'She is an ocean-going, forty-two footer with an enormous lead keel. I am more than confident she is capable of getting us over the channel. Not only that, but I have been on the sea more than on land most of my life. Yes, it will be a rough one, and you might not get your sea legs for a while, but at least no one will be trying to kill you.'

Jayne said she wasn't sure whether she would prefer facing an armed man or a raging sea. 'At least I would be able to control the situation better!'

Josh asked them if they would rather stay in dock, but they knew they had little choice.

'The thing is, Josh, there have been three deaths in as many months, two of which can most definitely be attributed to Jayne and me. The police will without doubt be scouring the area and will be able to pick up our scent in a short space of time. Once in police custody, we would be prevented from clearing our names. That would leave it all to Murky to try for us.'

They also knew that if they got released on bail, whoever wished them dead would be far more wary and plan their demise much more carefully.

'The next time they try, I can't see how they would fail. And added to that, Jayne is now involved, which is a whole new dimension. I know she is more than capable in any frontal attack, but next time they will use stealth.'

Josh was taking it all in and said that he understood the need for expediency. The moment the *Charlotte* was fully able; they would slip their mooring and head for France.

They drank a few more cups of tea and turned in, setting an alarm for five thirty. It was a most uncomfortable sleep to begin with because the *Charlotte* was rocking a lot, but after a while, the motion became more relaxing, and finally they both dozed off.

Everyone was woken up by a dreadful scream.

George and Josh were out of their bunks in a flash, and they tried to focus their eyes to see what had happened. As they turned around, they saw Jayne with her head cupped in her hands, sobbing.

George went across to comfort her, and she gradually became more lucid.

'I had a terrible dream, George. The man who attacked me had come back to life, and I wasn't able to get away.'

'You're all right now, my darling, I did wonder at how well you were taking it all. Training in unarmed combat is one thing, but to actually kill for the first time does tend to play on the mind.'

Jayne knew George had killed before and often wondered how he had dealt with it, but she felt it was something he was reluctant to talk about. George went on.

'The first time I ever experienced someone being killed were two chaps called Ndulu and Abdulla, who died protecting Stuart and me from two absolute horrors called Jürgen and Klaus. They too died as they were about to catch us along with all the men with whom they were associated.'

'Is that when Danny Knight and Hendrik Van Hove rescued you?'

'It was, poppet. But the worst thing was the carnage associated with our rescue. Danny, Hendrik, and their troops completely wiped out the rebel camp, and apart from the two Germans, they were really lovely people. They were all very friendly and jovial, sharing their food with us as if we were old comrades. Hendrik summed it up by saying that one man's terrorist is another man's freedom fighter. Although it made sense at the time, as the years have gone on, I have had time to reflect on it more, and it still bothers me. I know you have often wondered whether or not I killed anyone before all this happened, and I will tell you my first time of actually killing someone was a few years later in Kosovo. Having said that, I would rather not elaborate on the things that I have done. I feel that I was doing my duty, and I had to do a lot of terrible things for the greater good. Anyway, enough said. Let's try to grab some sleep, because we have a long day tomorrow.'

The rest of the night was peaceful, and when the alarm went off, they got to their feet. Jayne put on the kettle so they could have a hot drink.

'I won't put up any sails until we are out of the harbour, so it will be a bit relaxed. The wind isn't too bad in the Solent, and for the first part at least, we will have an easy day of it.'

The voyage from Hardway to the harbour entrance was very pleasant, but it was clear that outside, it was a bit choppy.

'We'll need to get closer inshore and use the back eddies to get out. The tide courses in quite fast when in full flow.'

Finally, they emerged into the Solent. Josh turned the *Charlotte* into the wind and asked George to take the helm and keep it steady. Josh then went forward to hoist the foresail first, followed by the mainsail. 'I'll keep all the sail area up because it will give us a good speed. *Charlotte* can handle a force five quite easily.'

Once all the sails were up, Josh took the helm, and instantly *Charlotte* heeled over picked up speed. They were close hauled and tacking, making their way towards Bembridge Ledge and, from there out into the English Channel.

Josh was in his element and clearly enjoyed the wind and sea spray that occasionally burst over the gunnels. 'It's oilskin weather on the foredeck,' he shouted. 'Or should I say foreskin weather on the oil deck.'

Both Jayne and George were surprised at how exhilarating the experience was, and although they were safely in the cockpit, Josh insisted they wear life jackets and harnesses.

They made good time and reached Bembridge Ledge in forty-five minutes despite having to tack all the way. Once they cleared the eastern edge of Bembridge, as Josh had expected, they were no longer in the lee of the island. Josh told George to take the helm and steer into the wind so he could reduce some of the sail area. He hoisted the storm jib and took in two in reefs on the mainsail because Jayne was looking a bit worried. 'Worry not, my dear. You are in safe hands! How is your stomach feeling?'

Jayne said she wasn't feeling seasick, but she was a little bit scared of the sea.

'I don't know about you but I could use a hot drink. Would you be kind enough to put on the kettle? George and I will keep you safe.'

They were making good progress, and although at times it was a little unnerving, Jayne managed to cope reasonably well.

After about six hours, Josh estimated that they were about halfway. With any luck, they would arrive around about six or seven in the evening. 'I am taking you to a little inlet at Le Touquet, and Étaples isn't very far from there. I will take you to meet the family once I have moored. They are a lovely couple called Iain and Steph Erkinshaw, and you will be safe from any prying eyes. In fact, if you need anything like a car, I'm sure they will get it for you. If you get caught, they can always say you stole it. You'll just be in a bit more shit than you're in at the moment.'

Jayne was naturally curious as to how Josh knew the couple, and he explained that they friends of his and Murky's families.

'We used to visit them when they lived in Gloucester. They're a very amenable couple. Iain always used to get into trouble with Steph for pulling faces behind her back, or doing something he shouldn't and blaming Murky and me for it.'

They laughed, and Jayne felt a little more relaxed because she was getting her sea legs, much to her relief.

After about half an hour, George looked behind and said that the sky looked really angry. 'We'll need to keep an eye on it. It could turn very nasty.'

Within a short space of time, the sky was illuminated with lightning, followed by a thunderous roar.

The storm was approaching at an alarming rate, and Josh said to George and Jayne that they should take the helm to try to keep the yacht on as even a keel as possible. Josh then went forward to lower the mainsail.

'We can still weather the storm, and the jib should keep us roughly on course.'

As he went forward, without warning the storm hit with a tremendous force. The sky was blacker than the darkest night, and visibility was down to just a few feet. George tried to keep an eye open for Josh, to make sure he was safe, but the combination of driving rain and heavy winds made it very difficult. Once Josh had stowed the mainsail on the boom, he carefully went forward to see make sure the jib was coping alright. George could barely see the bows of *Charlotte* from the stern, but he was able to make out the silhouette of Josh as he struggled with his ministrations. Finally satisfied, he started to make his way back towards the cockpit; it was clear he found it difficult. The waves were huge and crashed into the side of *Charlotte,* constantly making the situation precarious on deck, but Josh seemed to be managing it, just. The atmosphere was eerie and frightening; the sea was as black as ink, apart from the phosphorous and effervescent whiteness of the tops of the waves. They towered above the yacht, which was being tossed around like a cork.

Josh was now heading carefully back to the cockpit when a freak wave hit the *Charlotte* just as he released his grip to jump in. This caused him to briefly stand, and George saw the boom swing dangerously across the deck.

He tried to shout a warning, but the wind was so strong that it took the words out of his mouth, blowing the warning helplessly out to sea.

The boom cracked hard against Josh's upper arm and threw him unceremoniously over the side. The drag on the yacht was noticeable despite the fact that there was very little forward movement. George and Jayne reacted immediately, grabbing Josh's harness and trying to haul him back in, but the strain was enormous. Many times Josh was seen to disappear under, his pain-wracked body struggling to keep his head above water. The fight to save Josh was taking so long that there was a great deal of concern. Jayne's and George's hands ached with the strain and cold, but they used their last reserves to get him within grabbing distance – only to see him fall back in. George shouted at both Josh and Jayne to make one last-ditch effort to work together. Despite their near total exhaustion, they managed to finally grab the straps of his harness. By now, Josh was able to assist them as the pain began to subside in his arm, aided by the numbness he felt because of the cold.

Jayne took a quick look at it, and mercifully it didn't show any signs of a break, but she told him he would be getting quite a bruise. 'Right. You need to get out of those wet clothes before you get pneumonia,' she said as she ushered him down into the cabin.

George tried hard to keep the sails trimmed. The wind was gusting in different directions, but he seemed to be coping reasonably well.

The storm was still raging when George heard a slightly different sound, like a rhythmic thumping coming from his port side. Josh, who had just got into dry clothes, heard it too. He jumped back in to the cockpit and tried to start the engine in a panic, but it wouldn't start.

'What's the matter?' asked George, who clearly sensed something was wrong.

'We are right in the middle of the shipping lane, and we need to be able to manoeuvre ourselves under power.'

He tried several more times as the thumping became ever louder, but the engine refused to cough into life.

Jayne, not fully comprehending the gravity of the situation, asked whether the engine was usually this unreliable.

At first Josh was reluctant to answer, but after seeing the worry beginning to show in her face, he replied that in his haste to get it running, he may have flooded it. He tried to sound as reassuring as possible while struggling to get under steam.

The situation was now becoming extremely urgent because the sound of the approaching ship indicated that it was dangerously close.

Out of the gloom, the sinister dark shape of a hull appeared, and was it rapidly bearing down on them.

The three of them looked on in horror as the harbinger of their doom approached. They knew there was nothing they could do to prevent it.

Josh quickly grabbed a flare, but owing to the numbness in his hands, he dropped it and watched in horror as it bounced off the gunnel and into the sea. There were seconds before impact, and as a last result, he grabbed the torch to signal the bridge and try to alert the captain. He knew that he couldn't possibly alter course, but he hoped that if it was seen, they might alert the authorities. It was a pathetic gesture, but it was all they had.

'Oh, God!' Josh shouted as he made his way to launch the life raft. He knew it would be too late to avoid them getting smashed to pieces, but he thought they might have a chance of survival if they could get to it in one piece.

As the ship approached to within a few feet, the bow wave it was creating, together with another freak wave, lifted *Charlotte* and tossed her slightly away from a head-on collision. Then seconds later, it struck.

Although not head-on, the sound of impact was sickening as *Charlotte*'s gunnels scraped along the side of the ship.

After what seemed an eternity, the ship had passed, and they sat silently, stunned, amazed, and relieved that they hadn't actually been ripped apart.

Finally after composing himself, Josh went over to the side of impact and was satisfied that she hadn't been holed. 'She has sustained quite a bit of mutilation, but we are still in business, and the insurance will take care of the damage.' He then went back to the engine, which immediately fired into life. They were on their way again.

Once they had all settled, Josh began to feel the pain in his arm. He had all but forgotten about it in the excitement of the past hour, but now he felt a little nauseous. He showed Jayne how to use the various aids to find their position, and he told George to head on a bearing for Le Touquet. Then he went below for pain killers and a lay down. 'Wake me in about an hour, because I need to take control as we near France.'

The sea was beginning to get calm, and within the hour, after the last rumbles of thunder subsided, the storm had passed, exposing a lovely, warm, late autumn afternoon.

After all George and Jayne had experienced in being so close to death, they sat together quietly, feeling more at peace with the world than they had ever felt before.

Josh by now was feeling a little better as the combination of rest and pain killers took effect. He wandered into the cockpit to check on their progress. Jayne went below to prepare some hot drinks, and Josh told her where the bottle of rum was kept. 'I think we will have a good shot in all our coffees, to sustain us through to our destination,' he said. He was decidedly more upbeat, and although he was not in as much pain, he knew that once at the house in Étaples, he would need to convalesce for a while.

The remainder of the voyage was uneventful, and they managed to reach their destination and berthed at the marina in Port de le Touquet just after five thirty in the evening. Josh went to pay for the berth, stating he had sailed solo so that both George and Jayne could remain anonymous. He hoped beyond hope that the authorities wouldn't inspect *Charlotte*, and luckily they didn't. Having seen Josh's injury, they allowed him to return to *Charlotte* to change and get his arm seen to at a hospital.

They waited until after dark, took their chance to leave the marina unnoticed, and made their way to Josh's family friends. There, they knew they would be safe and could relax for as long as they needed.

CHAPTER 4

AT THE SCENE of the accident, Murky worked tirelessly to help the injured passengers in the vehicles involved in the pile-up. There were three in total, but by far the one sustaining the most damage was the one that ran into the back of Murky's van.

His total experience was limited to combat first aid, but it was enough to make the injured more comfortable. Within a short space of time, the sound of sirens became louder, and the first on the scene were the police followed a few minutes later by an ambulance.

Murky reported to the police officer to explain what aid he had given, and he added that he would like to speak to him about a totally unrelated matter. He explained that he had just heard the news he was wanted for questioning regarding the O'Rourke's disappearance.

The officer told him that unless he was wanted on criminal grounds, he would rather not deal with it right now because of the pressing issues at hand.

It took several hours to get everything moving again. Although badly damaged, the van was still safe to drive.

The passenger in the car behind Murky whose face had hit the windscreen had been seriously hurt with suspected spinal injuries. He was airlifted immediately to the Queen Alexandra's Hospital Portsmouth, to be operated on as soon as possible. Murky was naturally concerned and was told it was possible that the person may have a chance to be saved, but it was not certain whether or not he would have the use of his legs again.

Finally, before Murky was allowed to drive his van away, the police wanted to take all his details. It was then that the police officer realised the significance of who he was talking to.

Murky explained that he had been away on a survival holiday and had just heard he was required for questioning. 'In fact, officer, I am just on my way to report to my commanding officer before going straight to the station.' He went on to explain he was in the armed forces and was a staff sergeant.

Once Murky had shown his ID, the officer was satisfied and allowed him to drive away. As good as his word, he reported directly to the major's office and waited outside to be called in.

'Come in, Staff, and take a seat.'

Murky marched in and snapped to attention, but Major Bradley stood him down, reiterating that he should take a seat.

'Well, David, I know what has happened to George and Jayne, but fill me in on the latest developments. How are they both fairing?'

Murky took a deep breath and told him about their flight to Bristol, adding that his old van had broken down. He went on to explain how he had arranged passage to a safe house in southern France, but he wasn't sure whether they made the connection with his friend Josh because of the accident.

'An elderly couple reported that they had picked them up and said they were forced to drive them to Gosport. It would appear they made it all right, and the police have said that they had information suggesting they had gone back to the Isle of Wight. They have warned the public not to approach them because they might be dangerous, and a reward has been posted for any information leading to their arrest.'

'Oh, bloody hell. This is getting out of hand now,' Murky ventured.

Major Bradley asked whether Murky had an update on the situation, and whether George had any further ideas as to why someone was trying to kill him.

Murky explained about his run through Anne's Hill cemetery and what George now believed was some suspicious activity just inside the grounds. He went on to tell the major about the Daimler Jaguar, which was basically all they had to go on.

Major Bradley looked pensive for a while and said;

'Well, that is something to go on. Now, all we have to do is devise a way to investigate this in our own way – in-house, so to speak.'

'There may be a problem with my version of events, sir, because if George and Jayne were picked up a short distance from the A34, the police will have more than a strong suspicion that I got them that far. I would appreciate any advice you can offer!'

The major thought again and finally suggested that although the police would be suspicious, they also had no proof. 'I suspect you will be warned that it is a criminal offence to aid and abet, but if, for example, your vehicle gets a thorough cleaning inside and out ...'

He trailed off, and Murky immediately realised what he was getting at. The police would know that because he was in a different van, and if he was telling the truth, there would be no evidence of Jayne or George. If the police were to impound his van, their DNA would be all over it. He approached a few of his colleagues to give him a hand and get it scrupulously clean. He knew that if it was too clean, there would be awkward questions, so he had all his friends jump in once the cleaning was finished and basically wreck the inside again.

Once it had been done, he reported back to Major Bradley to request leave to report to the local police station.

'I think we'll have them come on to our territory to interview you, David. They need to know that you are going under cover for that assignment we discussed before you went on leave. As far as I'm concerned, national security outranks this situation by a long shot.'

Murky had been briefed before taking leave that he was to infiltrate a far-right group calling themselves the Urban

Commando Party, which had recently emerged apparently from nowhere. They were a violent and secretive group prone to carrying out acts of violence against people from organised crime syndicates. Very little was known about them or their leadership, and so far no charges had been brought to bear against any perpetrator of violence. The only thing they did know was that they had links with other criminal organisations around the world, and they were clearly being funded by a wealthy sponsor.

The major offered more advice regarding Murky's next move regarding clearing George's name, and then he reached for the phone.

That afternoon, two plainclothes police officers were ushered into the interview room, where Murky sat waiting with the major. The older officer introduced himself as Detective Inspector Edward Grimshaw and Detective Constable Mike Parbel.

Once they were asked to be seated and were made aware of all the domestics, the officers began their interrogation. They had to be reminded several times that Staff Sergeant Murphy was not involved in the any of the three killings and was therefore not a suspect.

'He only helped a friend and his wife because he thought their lives were in danger. He has assured me that once he dropped them off in Oxford, he had no idea where they were going, and he told them he didn't want to know.'

The younger of the two officers was quite a noxious fellow and was extremely aggressive. 'Oh, and why was that? So you didn't have to answer any awkward questions? I call that aiding and abetting a murder suspect!'

His colleague touched his elbow and asked in a lower voice, 'Are you aware that they were thumbing a lift along the Morestead Road? That isn't far from where you were involved in the accident, was it, sir?'

At first Murky didn't answer because his mind was racing to look convincing with his response, but just as he was about to open his mouth, the aggressive one almost spat out, 'I suppose that you are going to tell me that you have no idea what they were doing there, aren't you?'

Murky pretended to be totally shocked at this revelation. He looked at the major and then at the officer. 'I had absolutely no knowledge they were so close – and if I did, I will be honest and tell you I *would* have picked them up.'

The interview went on for some time with the good cop, bad cop routine, resulting in the two officers becoming increasingly agitated. The noxious one appeared to have taken quite a dislike to Murky, becoming more aggressive and threatening in his attitude. He began eyeballing Murky as he pointedly ceased asking questions, suggesting instead his own version of events. He was trying to put words into Murky's mouth.

Murky wasn't fazed at all by the attitude but met his glare. 'My grandfather fought in a war so that I didn't have to fear men in dark uniforms. I am cooperating and giving answers to the best of my knowledge, and your attitude is, quite frankly, disgraceful.'

The officer took no notice of what had been said and continued his tirade, seemingly oblivious to his colleague's attempts at calming down the situation.

Although appearing angry, Murky was not intimidated in the least and kept a cool head whilst giving measured answers to the incessant questioning.

Finally, the police told Murky he was to make himself available for questioning in the near future, and that he was not permitted to leave the camp. They also requested the keys to his van in order to carry out forensic tests.

With that, Major Bradley requested they remain seated while he made some phone calls.

'Hello, Emma. This is Charles Bradley. I know you are aware of the situation regarding George O'Rourke and Staff Sergeant Murphy, and you no doubt recall the briefing I gave you regarding the Staff's next deployment.'

The two officers sat in their seats, listening but clearly not understanding where this was leading. They could hear the sound of a female voice at the other end responding, but it was not audible enough for them to hear.

'I have two police officers present who wish to keep the Staff under near house arrest, but I need you to speak to them and explain that under the circumstances, that won't be possible.'

He beckoned the officer who appeared to be the most senior. The man took the phone and said, 'Good day, madam. I am Detective Inspector Edward Grimshaw and would reiterate the need to have Staff Sergeant Murphy at hand for further questioning, and he needs to make himself available accordingly!'

He listened to her response and said that although he understood what she was saying, he respectfully suggested that he didn't know who she was and could be the major's secretary.

There then ensued an exchange of words, and the detective inspector gave the name and contact details of his immediate superior before returning the phone to its cradle.

'Apparently, Ms Emma Belchin has requested that we return to the station and await word from the chief constable. She said she will ring you back, Major Bradley.'

The younger officer was about to protest but was restrained by DI Grimshaw, and they both left the office.

'Right, David. I have to say, that young police officer is what gives our superb police force a bad name. However, we have some time to discuss where we go from here. You are still officially on leave for a few weeks, so I suggest you do remain in camp in the main, but try to get to the bottom of George's predicament if you are able. It might be prudent to see how many black Daimler Jaguars manufactured in 2000 are around the area, and take it from there.'

Murky left the office and was really fired up, but he kept a level head, realising that if he was to be of any use to his friends, he had to find ways to conduct some sort of covert investigation.

The only real chance he had was to contact his brother, but he felt that for him to do it so soon after the police had left would look highly suspicious.

Sadly, an opportunity presented itself about a week later. Murky was called in before the CO again, who stood and ushered him to a seat.

'I won't beat about the bush, Murky.'

Murky knew something was wrong because the old man rarely ever referred to his subordinates by their nick names.

'I'm afraid that your father has had a heart attack and is in hospital. Your mother rang earlier, requesting that you go home to be with the family.'

'How bad is he, sir?'

'I'm afraid I don't know, but you are free to go when you are able. I realise that the police have impounded your car, so I am not sure how you will get there, but I can arrange a travel warrant for you to catch the train. The duty driver will take you to the station.'

'Thank you, sir. I will take the train, and I expect my brother will pick me up at the other end. I actually do have another car, a decent one.'

The journey to Alton took longer than expected due to delays, but he met his brother at the station after ringing him to give his estimated arrival time. He didn't think it prudent, and neither was it his first priority, to broach the subject regarding the black Jaguar. At that moment, he was more concerned about the state of his father's health.

Much to his relief, it was only a mild attack, and his father's life didn't appear to be in danger.

As soon as the car pulled up outside his parents' house, he rushed in to be with his mother, who was in a flood of tears.

'I really thought I was going to lose him, but thank God he is going to pull through. Thank you both for coming straight away, boys. I do appreciate it.'

Once all the fuss had settled down, Murky and his brother poured themselves a drink, sat down, and chatted. Their mother had explained that they wouldn't be able to visit their father until the morning, and so they asked about each other's activities of late. Murky's brother, Ethan, said that they had adopted a new approach with their 'stop and search' practice by not being so aggressive. On the face of it, it proved to be successful. Then he asked Murky how he was doing.

Murky delicately broached the subject of the black Daimler. 'It's a 2000 model, and I need to trace the owner.'

Naturally, Ethan was curious as to why, and so Murky told him about secreting George and Jayne away.

'Ah! Yes, I am aware that your friends – and of course you – you were wanted for questioning. I was contacted by the Hampshire police asking whether or not you had been in touch with me. They even came and questioned Mum and Dad, asking when they had last heard from you. So what does this have to do with the Jag?'

Murky was a little hesitant, knowing that Ethan was obliged to keep within the law, but he was put at his ease.

'It's all right, bro. If you couch your words carefully and don't tell me too much, I won't be in breach of conduct because I won't know anything.'

'George hasn't really got a clue what it's all about, but he has obviously seen something that he is not aware of, and as a result, someone is trying to kill him. We had a brainstorming session, and the only thing he can think of was when one evening he was running through a graveyard and thinks he saw something strange going on. At the time, he thought nothing of it. The only other thing he can bring to mind is the black Daimler Jaguar, which has a Y registration. There can't be too many around, and I hope we can resolve it fairly soon because I have loaned them some money. I only have a bit more they can borrow, but they won't be getting paid in their absence – and even if they were, their accounts will be watched closely for any activity. That would give away their whereabouts.'

'Do you know where they are, then?'

'Actually, I do, but I won't tell you because what you don't know, you won't have to lie about. It wouldn't be fair to you.'

'Okay, I will look into it and get word back to you. But I have to say, I can't be involved any further than giving you this information, and you didn't get it from me. Agreed?'

Murky nodded, and they carried on chatting about other things.

As the evening wore on, Ethan had an idea. 'Are George and Stuart still good friends?'

'I don't know. Why do you ask?'

'If they are, I know Stuart and Katy have been touring America. Apparently, the Americans have fallen madly in love with them. It has been reported that they are turning over hundreds of thousands of pounds a year in earnings. Not only that, but Stuart has just written a book, and it has gone viral. I believe they made their first million a few years back. Maybe they could help out financially?' He then put his hand up, indicating that he hadn't just said that.

It did set Murky to thinking because if it did ever come to a prosecution, they would need the best lawyers they could get.

The following morning, Murky and Ethan went to visit their father, who was sat up in bed, looked very chirpy, and gave them a big smile.

Their mother was ushered to the nurse's station, where she got an update on his condition and was told he was doing extremely well.

'It is likely that he will be home again in a few days. We would like to keep an eye on him for a while yet, but he has recovered well.'

They stayed until the end of visiting hours and made their way out to the car when Murky glanced over and thought he saw a familiar face. It was lost when an ambulance went by, obscuring his view. Murky was puzzled momentarily but thought nothing more of it until they arrived back at the family home. He suddenly realised who it was. Murky asked if he could use the phone to ring his boss.

'Hello, sir. It's Staff Sergeant Murphy. I thought you ought to know that I think the police officer who was conducting the interview is stalking me!'

It was obvious that the voice at the other end wanted clarification, and so Murky told him it was Parbel. He listened a short while longer before finally putting down the phone.

His brother naturally asked what it was all about, and Murky explained how rude one of the interviewing officers had been. The man had somehow found out where Murky was.

'The thing is, Ethan, I am about to do a job where this idiot could seriously endanger my mission. I won't trouble you with the details, and no need for you to worry. I know my boss will sort it out.'

With that, they settled down to catch up with how they were getting on, and whether Murky had decided when he was going to leave the army. It was something that he was thinking about, but the job excited him and was too much of a draw.

They chatted until late evening before retiring to their respective rooms, and they woke up the next morning to a hearty breakfast.

After three days, their father was allowed home with a strict regime that would be overseen by their mother. Both brothers felt it was safe enough for them to return to their respective professions.

When Murky had returned to barracks, the CO called him in and told him that he had taken it on himself to write to Stuart, explaining the situation and asking whether he could help.

'George has been an incredibly good operative and has got me out of one or two tight corners over the years. I also felt that if the police were vetting any mail you may be sending out, it was better coming from me, don't you agree? Oh, and one other thing. I reported DC Parbel to our Ms Belchin, and she has assured me that if either of those officers – or any other officer, for that matter – should interfere with you again, they would all face very serious charges. So now your deployment will be free of problems, God willing.'

Murky thanked him and left, hoping that something would materialise either from Ethan or Stuart before he had to depart for his next job.

CHAPTER 5

STUART AND KATY had been touring America for three years and were close to exhaustion. It was one of the longest gigs imaginable, and they decided it was time to take a break and return to England. The American public were in raptures whenever they were introduced to perform. Katy had developed a sense of humour that appealed to the audience, and they were loved as a double act.

This wasn't how the tour had started, because only Stuart had initially been performing, but after six months into the tour, they were both invited on *The Late Show with David Letterman,* where her crisp English accent, her sense of humour, and her natural beauty endeared her to people.

Stuart had received Major Bradley's letter a few days earlier, and although it was a good reason to declare their return to England, the decision had been thought about very seriously for quite a few months. Once he had read the letter, Stuart passed it over to Katy, who was naturally very worried.

'He is wanted for questioning about three murders? I don't understand. George was never criminally minded.

There has to be something more than meets the eye. Major Bradley seems to think we can help, but the only assistance we can give is to get money to him somehow. I hate to ask, Stuart, but can we get money to him to help him out?'

'George is one of my oldest and dearest friends, sweet. If there is anything we can do to help, we will somehow make it happen.'

Their very last appearance before leaving the States was to be invited back on David Letterman once again. It was said that the viewing figures rocketed a few minutes before the show was aired.

They arrived at the studio and were ushered to their dressing room. Their faces were lightly dusted with powder to prevent glare, and they were then taken to the wings to await their introduction.

'Ladies and gentlemen, the moment you have all been waiting for – and a sad one it is too. They have blessed us with their presence for three years and have now decided to go back to the old country, which we hope will not be forever. Please put your hands together and give a warm American welcome to Stuart and Katy Baxter.'

The applause was deafening, and they were both honoured with a standing ovation. The welcome went on for several minutes and then faded.

'Well, have we said something to upset you?' they were asked in a humorous way.

'I imagine the question is because we are returning to the UK. And no, you haven't, but we have been away for three years and need a break because it has been very tiring. We can't begin to tell you all how much we will miss America and all of you. You have been so kind to us,' Stuart said.

This set the audience to cheering and clapping again.

'Well, we will certainly miss you too, and we hope you both come back sometime in the near future. Anyway, your book, *By the Seat of My Torn Pants* – what inspired you to write it?'

'It stems back to my childhood with Katy's brother, George, and another good friend of ours, Ben. We were called the terrible trio and always seemed to get into trouble. As much as we tried to avoid it, it always seemed to catch us out. It was almost as if God was watching us all the time; we had been given this on good authority by our parents. Some of the things we did with pyrotechnics would get us into a lot more trouble these days, but making our own guns and bombs was too much fun to resist.'

'Ah! So it is biographical, then?'

'In part it is, but I have also added a lot of pepper and salt to the narrative, to give it a taste of humour.'

'Well, you have certainly achieved that. When I read it, I couldn't stop laughing.'

Stuart said, 'I'm glad you enjoyed it, but there are parts of it that I felt uncomfortable writing. For example, the inevitable bedroom scene where the hero sweeps his girl up in his arms to carry her to bed was a bit difficult to write, because I am not really in touch with my feminine side.'

'Ah! Was this based on a personal experience?'

'Well, I tried to do that with Katy, but once I reached the top step, I dropped her and knocked her unconscious. She doesn't remember a thing, but I had a whale of a time.'

Katy chirped in, 'Swept me up in your arms? Why don't you tell the audience who carried whom over the threshold after our honeymoon! You were too drunk, my sweet.'

'I had to pluck up courage to marry you, and don't forget, I still respected you in the morning!'

The audience laughed and applauded, and after about half an hour, their stint was over. They were once again given a standing ovation and left the studio. They got into a car that took them to the airport to fly back to Washington D.C.

They were not due to fly home for a couple of days, and they welcomed the peace and tranquillity of being together. They started to plan how to get money to George and Jayne without letting the authorities know where they were.

With their bags packed, they left for Dulles Airport and flew home.

CHAPTER 6

TWO DAYS AFTER Murky left his parents' home, Ethan made contact with him discretely in the form of a letter addressed to his CO.

Hi Dave,

Just wanted to let you know that I have managed to find some information for you. There aren't many cars that match the brief description you gave, so it narrowed the field down considerably. One in particular is and has been of interest to the Met and other agencies. It belongs to a known criminal, Charles Andrews, who is an associate of Afolabi Okorie. Okorie is a wealthy West African who, like Andrews, stays just on the right side of the law. Okorie has connections in every major city in Europe and is believed to run weapons, drugs, money laundering, and slavery. You name it, and he has probably got some interest in it.

A colleague of mine, Dudley Mortimer, was firmly ensconced in the case and repeatedly tried to bring charges against Andrews, but he was frustrated every time by a top-class barrister and technicalities. Dudley has since retired, and another operative has taken up the lead. Every attempt to infiltrate the group has failed, with each undercover officer mysteriously meeting fatal accidents. None of which, of course, can be associated with either Andrews or Okorie.

I realise this isn't the best news I can give, but I do have to say if these are the people your friend has inadvertently annoyed, they are the worst imaginable horrors that he could have picked.

Take care, Dave, and please don't do anything rash. I'm sure the authorities will manage to get them to justice in time.

It was good seeing you the other day; we should do it more often.

Best regards,
Ethan

Murky read the letter and sat down, thinking about how this had turned out to be the worst possible outcome.

'Staff, I don't really know what to say. I am sure you feel you need to involve yourself, but you haven't the time because of the next little shimmy you are scheduled to undertake.'

Murky answered the major by saying he felt he still had just over two weeks' leave left, and he would at least make some more enquiries. He had no intention of telling the major what he had in mind, because the less anyone knew about it, the greater the chance of him not being implicated.

He politely excused himself and left the office as he planned his next move. He knew what he planned to do was going to be in breach of the law, which could find him in prison for many years. He considered the situation long and hard until he finally decided that he was going to kidnap Charles Andrews. It would only be a matter of time before he extricated the information. Whether it would be done the hard or the easy way would be largely down to Andrews's resilience.

Knowing there wasn't enough time to plan the kidnap because Andrews would no doubt have a few bodyguards with him., he decided he had to take a chance and hope for the best

Murky set out his ideas in his mind, feeling that the first thing he needed to do was locate where Andrews could be found and quickly establish any patterns in his behaviour. It also crossed his mind that he would need a gun in the event he was compromised. This did worry him quite a bit. Using a firearm in the line of duty to defend the realm was one thing, but shooting someone on British soil was something else entirely. He realised that if that became the last resort, and he wasn't able to show it was in Britain's interest, not only would it be the end of his career and the loss of pension, but it would also mean a lengthy spell in prison.

He was aware that he would need a gun not associated with the armed forces, but he had contacts where he could acquire one.

As with anything he did, he would sit and plan the sequence of events, taking into consideration how little time he had. He also needed an accomplice, and he had two in mind. Both had since left the army; one now worked in a security firm, and the other had set up his own business. Both of them were firm friends of Murky and George because they had all served together in Bosnia.

Not wanting to expand this operation too widely, he decided to make contact only with Jonah, who was the most vicious of the four of them and would likely guarantee some results. Not many of Britain's enemies who had fallen foul of Jonah were able to withhold the information he wanted. He wasn't sadistic but would go to any lengths to defend the country he loved, and he was a devout royalist.

Murky went to Jonah's grocery shop in Fareham, where he and his wife had set up a flourishing business. Although his CO had assured him the police would not be following him, he took no chances, using well-versed tactics that would throw off any would-be tail.

'Hey, Jonah, how's business?'

'Murky! My God! How are you doing, and what brings you to my humble business?' Jonah rushed around the counter and gave him a big bear hug. 'Knowing you, you haven't come here for cucumbers, have you?'

'Is there somewhere where we can talk privately?'

Jonah looked at his wife, who smiled and gave him the thumbs-up.

They went through to the living room, which was quite a spacious, well-decorated room that clearly showed his wife's creative flair and good taste.

They sat down, and Jonah offered him a drink, but Murky said he preferred a cup of tea.

'So, old friend, what's this unexpected but very welcome visit about?'

Murky went into all the details and explained how he had managed to smuggle George and Jayne out of the country.

'So where are they now?'

'You are the only other person to know. A friend of mine took them over to France to a small village called Étaples. There is a retired couple there who are friends of my parents. They will have put them both up while I try to get to the bottom of it.'

'So, how do you think I can help? Would you like me to take some time out and join you? If so, you can count me in, but I would need to check with the missus.'

Murky explained the whole situation to him and added that he only had a very limited time in which to achieve a result.

'Okay, so what is your plan?' Jonah said.

'We have to separate a certain Charles Andrews from his heavies and get what information we can out of him.'

'Ah, interrogation – one of my specialities. Okay, getting him away from any minders shouldn't be too difficult unless they sleep with him. We know we are both able to get into a building, take who or what we want, and leave without making a sound. Is he married? If so, that will make life a little more difficult.'

'At the moment, I know nothing about him, so I'm not sure on the score. It doesn't leave a very big window of opportunity, and we have to move fast.'

With that, Jonah's wife Emma walked in. 'I have just shut up for lunch, if that's all right with your lordship,' she said with a smile.

'Emma, would you mind looking after the shop on your own for the next couple of weeks or so? Murky and George really need my help.'

Emma knew both George and Murky and was aware of George's situation. She said that she didn't mind at all but stopped short of asking what they intended to do. 'I can ask Matilda if she would like to earn a few extra quid and give me a hand in the shop.' Matilda was the daughter of Jonah's brother. She had left school and was on break from college.

'Right, we need to find where Andrews lives and take it from there. Would your brother be able to give details now that we have his car registration?'

'It's the only chance we have to make a start. I don't know if you heard, but my dad had a mild heart attack, and I met with Ethan while we visited our mum. He's the one who has already given me what little info I have, but I'm sure a little bit more won't compromise him too much.'

He phoned Ethan that afternoon, and by the evening, he received a text: 'Ring your CO.'

The following morning, Murky did ring, and the major confirmed he had received an email from Ethan simply giving an address near the New Forest. He also confirmed that Stuart had replied to his letter, having couched his words carefully. Stuart was pleased to help in any way he could.

Major Bradley said, 'They have both come back to the UK for a break and to meet up with family and friends. The help he has offered is to finance the case with as much money as it takes to get George and Jayne out of trouble. We have to work out how he will be able to make the funds available without raising suspicion. This is all highly irregular, and I don't want to be involved in it beyond all that I have done. Having said that, I know someone who is good at this kind of thing. Maybe he can sort it out.'

Murky thanked him and said he would try not to make contact with him again on this subject unless he really had to.

Jonah said, 'Well, it seems we're on a very tight schedule and will need information very rapidly, so I will get my little bag of tools.'

Murky asked Jonah about his methods and whether it ever pricked his conscious.

'As far as I am concerned, I hate hearing the screaming and seeing anyone in agony. Usually the sight of the contents in my tool bag is enough to frighten the information out of them. The way I see it, that anyone who would cause harm to an innocent person ceases to have any right to be called a human being. So in answer to your inferred question, no, I am not a sadist, and I don't enjoy it.'

They both readied themselves and left the shop after they had an early lunch at Emma's insistence. They arrived at the address that Ethan had given by mid-afternoon.

'Wow! His job must pay well!'

The property was set in a beautifully landscaped garden, and the house itself was barely visible because it was set in a forest of ash, oak and birch trees.

They decided to skirt the property for any signs of an easy point of entry. It took a couple of hours before they managed to find a possible opening by an adjoining piece of land that was essentially a continuation of the forest.

Taking a good look around and being careful not to set off any potential alarms, they spotted a network of CCTV cameras covering every inch of open space.

'Well, they will almost certainly have seen us, but I have a plan. Before that, we need to establish how many people we have to neutralise before getting at Andrews, and we also need to make sure he is in the residence.'

They decided to keep a constant surveillance on the property, with one resting while the other kept watch. It was something they were both used to doing in all weather, and they knew they would get some sort of result in a short time. The only worry that Murky had was whether he was barking up the wrong tree. If Andrews and his cronies weren't the culprits, he had no idea where to go from there.

They got back into Murky's van to keep a vigil near the entrance to the estate, parking the van in the most inconspicuous place. They waited for an hour before they were rewarded by the gates swinging open automatically, followed shortly after by a black Daimler Jaguar driving into the grounds.

They weren't able to see the registration number from their position, but Murky felt it was too much of a coincidence that a Daimler should be arriving at this address, even if they didn't know who was inside yet.

'This looks promising. We may be able to catch him while he's in!'

They decided to wait until it got dark before they ventured in, and so they settled down, planning their moves once they were in. They had no idea how many people were in the estate or whether there were any dogs running around, but both felt confident they were more than capable of neutralising any threats.

It was an hour after dark when the car doors were thrust open, and two men stood on either side of the car, brandishing guns.

'Well, well, ladies. What have we got here?'

Murky managed to hide his shock but was very annoyed with himself for assuming he wouldn't be caught out. He had never been this clumsy before and vowed silently that it would never happen again. He said, 'What's your problem, and what the hell do you think you're doing? Just close the doors and disappear before I get out and show you the way!'

'Oh, you are both getting out and coming in with us. Don't worry about that!' This was said menacingly as the men pointed their guns at Murky's and Jonah's faces.

It was no use protesting, but as Murky was about to leave his side of the car, he nudged Jonah and nodded. It was a silent way to let his friend know he intended neutralising them as soon as they got out. Jonah didn't need any prompting and knew exactly what to do and when to do it.

They both exited the car slowly and passively, to throw their captors off guard, and as soon as they were free of the car, they acted in unison.

They swung round, grabbing the hands holding the guns and catching both men off balance. In a flash, both men fell to the ground choking because of the straight-fingered punch to their Adam's apples. Removing the guns from their hands was easy because the men were trying hard to breathe. Murky had his assailant bound up like a Christmas turkey in a flash, and he went over to help Jonah. Jonah was kneeling next to the other attacker, and in a very calm but menacing voice, he asked how many others were inside.

'Go and stuff yourself. You won't even make ten yards before you'll be taken out!' the man replied.

Jonah removed a strange-looking tool from his bag and grabbed the man's little finger. He placed the tool around the little finger and told him it was his last chance. The man laughed, saying that they didn't know with whom they were dealing.

'Wrong answer!' Jonah squeezed the handles together and the little finger was cut away from his hand. The man screamed in agony and began to struggle violently, trying to break free, but he was being held down too tightly.

'Give me any more wrong answers, and you lose nine other fingers. Then I will really start to hurt you. Believe me, I really don't like doing it, but if I have to, I will take you apart piece by piece. Now, be a good chap. How many are there inside?'

The man spat at Jonah, who grabbed his index finger and cut that one off, causing him to scream again.

'You're crazy, man! Who are you? You're not the police. If you are from another gang, you'll all be taken out slowly and painfully. Trust me, you are in over your heads.' It was quite pitiful because he was now crying with the pain, and he was also afraid of what would happen next.

'Who are you and what do you want?' said the man whom Murky had trussed up.

'All we want is information, and then you can both go back home to your mummies. Now, I will only ask once more, and if you think your fingers hurt, it's nothing compared to what I intend to do next to your balls. If you make me put my hand down there – and believe me, I don't want to – you will end up singing like a soprano. For your sake, how many?'

'Okay, okay! Just keep those bloody clippers away, and I'll tell you.'

Jonah removed the device from around a finger and told him to start singing.

'There are three others, and some dogs.'

'Does that include Charles Andrews? If you're lying, whatever you ate at lunchtime will be your last meal. How many dogs are there?'

'Andrews has just come back from his meeting, and there are three dogs patrolling with the three men.'

'So that was him in the car. Now, that was less painful, wasn't it?

The man told them all they needed to know after realising they weren't amateurs and meant what they said. Once Jonah and Murky had all the information they wanted, they bound and gagged both men and bundled them into the car.

Realising that the men would be missed and expected back to the house soon, they drove the car away some distance and hid it down a dirt track, removing any signs as to its whereabouts.

Murky said, 'If they knew the car was there, it is almost certain that they would have seen it move. Even more likely, they would know their men have been neutralised. We need to act fast now and get in before they realise they are under attack.'

From the boot, they took their favoured weapons (a Fairbairn-Sykes and Glauca B1) and some rope, and then they blackened all exposed skin. Murky decided to leave the gun behind because although it did have a silencer, using a weapon *not* in the interests of the general public could end his career. They decided they would enter the grounds from two different locations. Murky would slide in to the front entrance over the wall where there were trees, and Jonah would go around to the side where they had found the clearing earlier that afternoon.

Both entered the grounds, but Murky fared better than Jonah. Within two minutes of entering the clearing, Jonah was seen, and one man accompanied by a fierce dog was heading in his direction at speed.

Jonah stood still and purposefully removed both knives. He waited until he considered he would be able to strike effectively. He adopted a stance where his whole body was well balanced, and he threw the Fairbairn-Sykes, catching the dog handler squarely in the chest. The man fell about twenty feet in front of Jonah, but the dog was now loose and growling angrily as it made for Jonah.

He quickly placed the Glauca in his right hand, exposing the blade. As the dog made a leap at him, he rolled with it, striking it in the soft skin just under the rib cage. The speed of the dog's forward motion and the strength of Jonah's strike made the blade cut in deep, spilling its entrails out of its abdomen. The dog let out a cry of pain and fell to the side, writhing in agony.

Jonah didn't like hurting animals, but he knew he had no choice. He quickly dispatched the dog, retrieved the Fairbairn from the dog's handler, and continued stealthily into the grounds. He estimated that it was about an acre in size with lots of cover, but he knew there would be other attempts to neutralize him.

As he was heading for the house, the hairs on the back of his neck prickled, and he realized he been seen because one of the other guards had the drop on him. It dawned on him that the person he extracted the information from might have lied, in which case he was in serious trouble.

'Let's see those knives thrown to the ground, and your hands in the air!' the man yelled.

He removed both knives from his belt and threw them on the floor, making a mental note of their whereabouts in case he got an opportunity to get the better of the guard. Jonah felt the cold nozzle of a gun thrust painfully into his neck.

'Move, and keep your hands where I can see them, or you will hit the floor like a sack of shit!'

Jonah began to move as he was told but pretended to stumble while reaching back to grab the hand. The guard was too quick. With a well-aimed strike, the man kicked Jonah in the back of his legs, causing him to fall on his knees.

'Last chance. Get up and keep moving Try that again, and you are a dead man!'

They entered the house, which was plush in the extreme and smelled quite sweet. Jonah was ushered into a large room, where a well-dressed gentleman in his forties smiled with a look that Jonah would take great pleasure planting his fist into. Jonah hoped beyond hope that Murky would somehow distract them enough to enable Jonah to gain some sort of advantage.

His hopes were dashed when he saw his friend being forced in at gunpoint a few moments later. It was clear that their movements had been observed almost as soon as they had dealt with the two heavies.

'Good evening, gentleman. I am Charles Andrews, and I suggest you sit down very carefully. I warn you now, these two are trigger happy, and we have enough grounds here to ensure your bodies will not be found for a century. Now, we can either do this the hard way or the easy way – your choice. Who are you, and what are you after?'

'My friend and I are from a group called the Urban Commando Party, and we are out to cause anarchy, especially with rich, successful people like you. We are going to bring the whole system down around your ears, and if you get rid of us, others will follow!'

Andrews looked pensive for a moment and began clapping. 'A gallant attempt, gentlemen, but because I don't recognise either of you, you have to be lying. I recruited most of the members of the Urban Commandos, so I think I should know who my men are. Speaking of men, you will suffer for killing one of them, but I will make it quick if you tell me the whereabouts of the two gentlemen I sent out to invite you in.'

One of the other guards walked up to Murky with a look of thunder on his face, and he shoved a gun into Murky's forehead. 'One of them is my brother, and it won't be quick if you have killed him!'

Getting so close to Murky was a fatal mistake. In the blink of the eye, he quickly pushed the gun hand to one side, Grabbing his arm, he spun the man around, pulling his arm under his own armpit so that the elbow was held firmly next to his side. He then jumped slightly and rammed both of them to the floor. The sound of bones breaking was sickening, and the man screamed in agony.

Jonah also acted as soon as Murky first moved his hand. In two huge strides, he closed the gap between himself and the other man, who was clearly shocked at what was happening and as a result was caught off guard. Jonah then spun around, delivering a debilitating kick to the man's groin. He too screamed in agony and fell to the floor.

Andrews looked on in horror as it dawned on him that the tables had been turned against him, and he tried to make a break for the door. He almost got it open when he heard the crack of a pistol, and wood splinters flew away six inches from his head. He stopped and turned to see that Jonah had picked up a gun and stood with a steady hand, pointing the gun at him.

'You're a lucky man – I was aiming for your legs. Now, come sit down. We need to ask you some questions. What was it you said? Ah, yes, that was it. We can either do this the hard way or the easy way. Which is it to be?'

Andrews looked around nervously for a way out. Upon realising he had no choice, he returned to his chair.

The man that Jonah had kicked was starting to get to his feet, but Jonah kicked him very hard in the face and again in the head. He was wearing heavy boots, so it rendered the man unconscious. There was no need to deal with his colleague because his arm was so badly broken that he was totally incapacitated.

They both walked to where Andrews sat, and he looked at them in fear. Beads of sweat dripped from his temples, and the furrows caused by the stress lines could have a crop of potatoes planted in them.

'What do you want? Money? I can give you enough, as much as you want.'

As they looked at Andrews menacingly, they noticed his face change briefly, and they heard a slight noise behind them. Murky reacted instantly, spinning around and closing the distance between himself and the man who was now recovering from the kicking he had received. 'You're a tough one, aren't you? Try this for size!' He aimed another kick but the man somehow managed to dodge it, and he attacked Murky.

Andrews looked furtively at the fight between Murky and his man, and then back at Jonah. He was clearly hoping Jonah would avert his gaze to see what was happening and take his chance, but Jonah didn't bat an eyelid. Jonah had no doubt about the outcome and stood rock solid, never taking his eyes off of the terrified man.

The fight only lasted a short while because the man had been badly hurt in the previous attacks, giving Murky the advantage. Murky would have won anyway, but it would have taken longer to render him incapable of any further action. Using his elbow when the opportunity presented itself, Murky put all his strength into a strike on the temple. The man fell to the floor lifeless. Murky didn't want to take any chances, and he sat his opponent up, wrapped his arm round the head, and broke the neck.

The sound wasn't lost on Andrews who was shaking wildly.

Murky and Jonah knew that silence was a good tool that could be applied to intimidate effectively, and so they stood directly in front of him with menacing looks. The longer they stood in silence, the more nervous Andrews got. Much to Andrews's annoyance, when he spoke again, his voice almost squeaked and broke, as if he was about to cry. He was clearly frightened. Suddenly he made to open a drawer, but Jonah raised his gun, tutting and shaking his head. Thinking better of it, the prisoner put his hands back on the table. Still his tormentors said nothing.

Jonah handed the gun to Murky, reached into his inner pocket, and produced a little package.

'Ah! Are we lopping off fingers again?' Murky asked.

Jonah shook his head and produced a packet, which he spread out over the desk. Inside was a selection of funny-looking needles. 'I think we need to clean out his fingernails, don't you?'

Murky wasn't well versed in Jonah's instruments of torture, although he knew his friend referred to them as tools of information.

They both walked slowly around the desk towards Andrews, who was looking at them in terror. Again he offered them more money than they had ever seen, enough to last them two lifetimes.

Still they said nothing, and Jonah started to remove Andrews's tie. Jonah told Murky to hold him down, and he tightly tied one of Andrews's wrists to the arm of his chair. He looked around for something else to tie the other hand.

'Wh-what are you going to do?' Andrews almost sobbed.

Jonah said, 'Ah! I see you are only as brave as the thugs you have protecting you. Now, you have a choice: you will tell us everything we want to know, or you can suffer. It's up to you!'

Murky walked to the henchman who lay dead and removed his tie. Just to be sure they would have no further interruptions, he went across to see the other man, but there was no need to worry. Every time the man moved, he winced in agony because his arm was hanging in an ugly fashion from his side.

Murky took the tie and tied Andrews's other wrist to the arm of the chair. He stood back as Jonah took the needles from their pouch and said, 'Now, then, where do we start?'

Murky started the questioning with his head no more than a few inches from Andrews's face. The prisoner was unable to hide his fear.

Jonah grabbed one of his fingers as Andrews struggled, to no avail. Jonah placed the needle just under a fingernail and nodded to Murky.

Murky said, 'Right, we want to know two things. First, you're going to tell me all you know about the Urban Commando Party. Next, why are you trying to kill a man called George O'Rourke?'

'I have never heard of him. You've got the wrong man!'

Murky looked at Jonah, who began to lightly push the needle a little further under the nail, but not enough to break the skin. Andrew screamed – not with pain because it wasn't inserted in deeply enough, but because he was filled with wretched fear.

'Let me try to refresh your memory. Your car was seen outside Anne's Hill Cemetery in Gosport, and you were involved in a killing that you think our friend had witnessed. Just for your information, he didn't see anything and the biggest mistake you made was trying to kill him.'

Andrews remained silent for a while; his face was a ghostly white.

As it turned out, Andrews was not at all a gallant man, and he begged not to be hurt, adding that he would tell them everything they wanted to know.

They began the interrogation by asking why there was an apparent contract out on George. Andrews explained that although he didn't know George's name, he was seen to be looking at what was going on in the graveyard. 'My boss had him followed to his house, and we waited for an opportunity to kill him. I'm sorry, but the top man isn't one to be messed with. When he says jump, we ask how high.'

'His name?'

Andrews hesitated, but Jonah wiggled the needle a bit, and the man shouted out that the name was Afolabi Okorie.

Murky said, 'The second question. Who are the Urban Commando Party, and what is your involvement with them?'

'Afolabi wanted to raise a group that would disrupt and cause chaos in and around the country as a diversion, especially with financial establishments, because he is planning something big.'

'You'll have to do better than that. Start singing, or my colleague will really hurt you.'

'Who the bloody hell are you, anyway? How do I know whether or not you work for Afolabi? He doesn't trust anyone and checks on all his people, to ensure their loyalty.'

'Wrong answer, and last chance. What is he planning?'

Andrew's remained silent, clearly not knowing what to say. Jonah pushed the needle under the nail a tiny fraction, and Andrews screamed once again. 'But I swear to you, I don't know what it is he has in mind! I'm not that high in his organisation. Please, you have to believe me!'

Murky placed a hand on Jonah's shoulder, who removed the needle and, much to Andrews's relief, placed it back in its pouch.

'I imagine you know that you are being monitored, and so you must have a means of communication outside of the public domain. An unregistered mobile, perhaps?'

Andrews looked a little reluctant at first, but when Jonah reached for the pouch, he nodded towards the adjoining room.

In there was an elaborate system of communications, and neither of them were familiar with any of it. Murky said, 'This is where either George or Ben would come in handy.' Ben had been the fourth member of the team, and he was experienced in communications.

They went back to where Andrews was still tied firmly to his chair, and they wheeled him in to the room.

'Right! I need a secure line where I know I won't be overheard, either by any of your cronies or the police. Do you understand the consequences you will suffer if you put the slightest foot wrong?'

In abject resignation, Andrews agreed to show them what to do. Now that he knew his tormentors were not with the police, he was very worried. He realised they couldn't be from a rival gang either, because they were far too professional. As far as he knew, hitmen only normally operated alone.

'Hello. Put me through to Major Bradley, please! It's Murky.' There was a short pause, and then the major answered. 'Hello, sir. I think we may have nailed two birds with one stone. We have confirmed it *is* Andrews who is at the head of the attempts at George's and Jayne's lives. He is also heavily involved with the Urban Commandos. I have Jonah here with me, but we need some assistance. We have two dead and two injured, and we have Andrews.'

The major sounded very pleased with the result and asked where to send the transport. Once it had all been arranged, they made doubly sure that neither Andrews nor the man with the broken arm could move by tethering them together. The badly injured man was difficult to move because it was clear they were hurting him when they dragged him towards the chair; he vomited with the pain. Instead, they dragged the chair to him and tied his good arm to the centre post.

Andrews complained that his hands were hurting, and although they were turning blue, neither Murky nor Jonah were prepared to release his bonds because they had to go out of the premises to bring in the van.

Once they had left the building, they walked back into the grounds to retrieve their weapons and make for the car.

It was a precaution for both of them in case their prisoners had managed to free themselves, but very few ever managed to do that once they had been tied up.

'How did you know about the Urban Commandoes?' asked Jonah.

Murky explained that it was going to be his next assignment. 'It couldn't have been more fortuitous, Jonah. This could prove to be George's salvation. If we can get Andrews to confess all using your methods can't be relied upon to extract information, we can hopefully get George and Jayne back home safely.'

Two hours later, the whole area had been secured, and all prisoners were whisked off for questioning.

Murky thanked his friend for his help and said that he could now return to being a green grocer. Jonah accepted the handshake and said that life would be fairly dull now that the bit of excitement was over. 'Murky, my dear boy, I would be more than happy to be called upon to work with you outside of the authorities and be like a fifth columnist. You only have to say the word.'

Murky said that he would certainly consider it because Jonah was still effectively on the reserve list.

Chapter 7

Josh, George, and Jayne had been with the Erkinshaws for three days, and Josh was almost fully recovered from his ordeal at sea. He had been back to the marina the day before to arrange maintenance to his yacht, which was being done through his insurance. He was told that it would take about a week for the repairs to be completed. George had offered money to his hosts, but they refused, saying that providing the two helped towards buying food, no payment was necessary.

In the days following Andrews's arrest, Murky had asked his CO if he could visit his parents to see how his father was getting on, but the main reason was to get a message to George. He dictated what he wanted his parents to send since things had yet to be cleared up, and George and Jayne were both still wanted by the police. Any suspicion as to the destination of the message could jeopardise what they wanted to achieve, which was to get Jayne and George out of danger and eliminate the chance of them being arrested.

Dear Iain and Steph,

I thought I would drop you a few lines to see how you are getting on, and I hope that this finds you both in good health. It seems such a long time since we last met, and we plan to come over for a few days later in the year, if that suits you.

Rumour has it that your son is paying you a visit at the moment. The last time we saw him, he asked Margaret's advice regarding his girlfriend. Ah, young love – I remember it well. Bless him!

If he is still with you, could you tell him that we bumped into Louise the other day, and she has said she has nearly ironed out all the things that were causing her problems; it should soon be all right for him to come home. She asked that he give her a little more time because she is planning a big surprise, and she will let him know when to come back. If he is there with you, tell him to hang on for a little while yet, and I'm sure we can have him reunited with his old life.

Take care, both of you, and we'll be in touch again soon.

Best wishes,
Bill and Margaret

'Do you think that he will understand the message, Dad?' Murky asked.

His father said that Iain was no fool. Besides, his son and girlfriend were planning a short visit later and planned to marry next year. 'If George is there,' he assured Murky, 'he will pass on the message, and I'm sure he will understand what is being said.'

Murky returned to base the following morning, pondering how to get to the bottom of it all. Although he now had Andrews in custody, the man would no doubt claim that anything he said was extracted under duress. It did cross his mind, however, that he wasn't with the police and that Andrews and his cronies were safely tucked away for the time being.

He reported to Major Bradley, who told Murky that whatever he and Jonah had done to him really loosened his tongue, and he was prepared to spill all.

'Having said that, Staff, we both know when it comes to a court case, and he is no longer alone in a dark interview room, he will most likely claim he was tortured. We really can't afford to have him running loose again. His freedom would most definitely compromise your ability to get to the bottom of the Urban Commandoes. It seems that they have become autonomous and are getting funded by an account that was put together for them by Afolabi Okorie and Andrews. We really need to get to the bottom of it because they are becoming very powerful. We don't know what Okorie is planning behind the smokescreen of their activities.'

Once the meeting with Major Bradley had finished, Murky picked up the secure phone to talk to Emma Belchin and bring her up to date with recent events.

'I think the time has come for us to put together a team to begin disrupting the UCP's activities. There is no need to infiltrate the group anymore because all previous attempts have ended with fatalities, but a small group of specialists could do some serious harm. We could begin with picking off small numbers at a time and using our special methods of getting information. I am thinking of bringing Jonah back into the fold temporarily, because it is in the nation's interest. I'd also like to get George back, but we will need to ensure the police don't get in the way. What do you think?'

'Two things, Charles. First, we will need the police on our side at some point, so I suggest we get back George and let the police know he will be working in the interests of the UK's safety; the very mention of Andrews or Okorie will immediately get their attention. Second, I cannot and will not condone the torturing of any prisoners; if I hear about it happening, there will be very serious consequences, so I am not expecting to hear about such barbaric methods. Do you understand?'

The major acknowledged her concerns and reassured her by saying that there were many methods of gaining information, and as a result she would not become aware of which methods were used. He also took the hidden meaning that he had a free hand providing no one was made aware of it. He knew he could get Jonah to extract whatever information he needed without the use of pain; that was normally a last resort, when time was short.

'One other thing, Charles. I know your preferred team size is four, but with so much interest by so many agencies, it is likely that the team might need to be larger.'

'How much larger? If it is too big, it will be difficult to manage, and I would really like Murky's group to be reinstated because of their individual abilities. The maximum that we could manage is perhaps one more, two at the most.'

Emma Belchin agreed that would be the best way forward, and she would see what she could do. Major Bradley finished the conversation and put down the phone.

The following morning, Charles Bradley had recalled Ben Jarvis from his current commitment to brief him before gathering the whole team and discussing a meaningful strategy. Ben was an expert in communications, but like the rest of his team, he had many other talents, such as demolition. He was the smallest of them all but was wiry and perhaps the most deadly in unarmed combat.

Bradley then contacted Murky to take steps in bringing George back from his hiding place, and also to touch base with Jonah to see if his offer to help still stood. He explained that it would be best if Jayne remained in hiding for the moment because of the uncertainty of what would happen next. Knowing that it would take some time to get the team back together, notwithstanding the need to give Emma Belchin time to make contact with the police regarding George's recall to active duty, he started making plans for the operation.

CHAPTER 8

MURKY WAITED UNTIL he got the all-clear before taking steps at getting George back to England. The word came three days later. Knowing that he had a free hand without fear of being followed by the police, he arranged a flight in a Piper Seminole and flew direct to Le Touquet Airport, where he told George to wait for him.

He had rung ahead to speak to the Erkinshaws and explained what was happening. He also spoke to Josh, saying he would arrange to have another friend join him and help crew the *Queen Charlotte* back to England at a time of his choosing. Not knowing how long it would be before Jayne could come out of hiding; he also asked Iain and Steph if they minded having her stay for a while longer. Since Stuart had made unlimited funds available, he was able to offer them money. At first they refused, but they were ultimately persuaded to accept it.

Things were now beginning to gather pace, and within five days the team was almost in place to begin upsetting the UCP. Before Charles Bradley went about setting up a briefing, he had a phone call from Emma Belchin requesting that she be invited to attend as well, because she had received significant intelligence. She didn't elaborate but said it would be best if the whole team were assembled so that she could brief everyone at the same time. Once Charles Bradley was aware that the team was available, he scheduled a meeting for two days later.

His office wasn't big enough to accommodate everyone, and so he booked a conference room where the team of four sat waiting for the remaining members of the group to arrive. While he was waiting, he warmly welcomed George and Jonah back into the fold, expressing relief that at last there was a good chance to return George and Jayne to a safe environment.

It wasn't long before the guard room rang to say that the guests had arrived, and Ben was asked to escort them to the meeting.

Emma Belchin entered the room with two other gentlemen, whom she introduced as Connor Lynott and Brendan Taylor, explaining that they were from MI6. Once all the introductions were out of the way, Charles opened the meeting and asked Emma to address the collective with the new intelligence that she had acquired.

'Good morning, gentlemen. We have had a minor breakthrough in identifying somebody whom we suspect as being in the pay of Afolabi Okorie. I'm afraid that it nearly goes to the top of the government, and whatever is being planned, we suspect that it could involve an attack of some sort on a senior member of the cabinet – perhaps more than one. Not only that, but as I will explain as I go on, it could also mean something entirely different.'

Naturally, everybody wanted to know more, especially where the information had come from. Nearly all present were firing questions when Charles Bradley put his hand up, bringing the meeting to order. 'We need to let Ms Belchin speak. She will more than likely cover all of your points, and we'll leave questions to the end, gentlemen. Right, Emma. Please continue.'

'We have had some suspicion about a senior ranking politician for some time. He was seen having a meal with Charles Andrews, who as most of you know has been of some interest to us for quite a while. It was a chance sighting by Connor here, who had been keeping an eye on Andrews, finding out more of where he went and what establishments he frequented. We gave him the false identity as the son of a rich, reclusive entrepreneur, enabling him to visit the same establishments without drawing attention to himself. He kept a very low profile, appearing not to be paying any attention to the other customers but passively observing. This went on for months when, one evening, Andrews walked in accompanied by MP Julien Algar, who is the supremo for the newly formed anti-corruption department. Since then, we have been intercepting messages from him, and one in particular got our immediate attention. It was sent directly to Okorie and blind copied to Andrews. At first it made no sense because all it said after all the usual niceties was, "Crossword clues to follow." The next message followed a week later and said, "Mail Friday 21 – 4 across."

We looked at the puzzle, and the answer was "prime minister". Naturally at first it didn't mean much, but as the messages began to flow, the clues came together to make "Prime minister following functions", and it went on to list a series of venues with the only common denominator being places that the prime minister will be attending in the next six months.'

'Do we deduce that we can expect some kind of an attack on the PM, then?'

'Well, this is the thing, Okorie is not a fool, but we believe he has used this sort of tactic before, where he has taken no chances in case by chance his correspondence is intercepted, and he has thrown in a few red herrings. The trouble is we believe he does this frequently; not just the one feint but several, which is why it has been impossible to pin anything on him. Everything he does is, on the face of it, totally innocent. He also mixes with the highest echelons of society. Prima facie, he is the epitome of a wealthy, successful businessman and an upstanding citizen of the community. As a result, intelligence agencies have been sent on wild goose chases, and while they were looking the other way, Okorie was masterminding the real crime. For example, in 1990 a financial messenger was mugged for £292 million in government bonds, very little of which has ever been recovered. It is suspected it was an inside job, but whereas the authorities were expecting to raid a warehouse full of illicit drugs, the mugging took place some miles away. All of Okorie's associates at that time were hauled in, but with no evidence, they all walked. More recently, in 2003 a similar situation in Antwerp occurred, where there was credible evidence of a huge arms deal, but it was yet another decoy. At the time of the raid, there was a massive diamond heist. I don't want us to become seduced away from what the real target might turn out to be. I think this time he is becoming overconfident because not only have we easily been able to decode these messages, but other correspondence from various sources have equally proved easy to decipher. Previous intelligence on many other crimes we believe he has orchestrated has been far more sophisticated. We do need to be vigilant on all the intelligence received, but we feel we may possibly have hit on the real target. In July, four diamonds are to be loaned to the British Museum for one month. They have all been offered by individual owners, and the total value is in the hundreds of millions. The diamonds are the Allnatt, the Ashberg, the Blue Moon of Josephine, and the Pink Star. It would be a dreadful situation if they were stolen, and it would cost this country a great deal in credibility. One other thing: whenever such a crime has happened in the past, Okorie's private yacht is usually in the vicinity. It's called the *Ardent Voyager*, and we now believe that it is used as an HQ to control operations.'

George thought about what had been said and told everyone present that he had actually been on board that yacht when he and Stuart had been kidnapped by a German arms smuggling group. 'In fact, as it turned out, the head of the group was an undercover West German intelligence officer called Bernhardt Von Austerlitz. I don't know the boat intimately because we were banned from certain parts, notwithstanding the need to hide from two horrors called Jürgen and Klaus. Do we have any indication as to when they will actually try to steal the diamonds? If we are able to get a specific day, Murky and I could get aboard somehow and disrupt proceedings.'

'Once again, we have to be sure that the diamonds are the real target, because it could be another feint. We are currently looking at all employees of the museum to see if there is a potential insider, but with all the high-tech gadgetry and high-profile security, it is difficult to see how they could achieve such a heist. What you and Murky could do George is to get on board anyway, to see what you can dig up. One other thing: we have been keeping an eye on Charles Andrews's estate, and it has been visited by one or two people whom we believe to be fairly senior members of the Urban Commandos. The absence of Andrews and his cronies will have raised suspicion. We are still very much in the dark as to Okorie's intentions, and the only thing we have to go on is what information we can glean from inside his yacht.'

With that, the meeting was closed. George and Murky would prepare themselves for their mission. Ben and Jonah would be nearby for back-up should it be needed, and Connor Lynott and Brendan Taylor would attempt to create a distraction in order to allow George and Murky to sneak aboard. No one had any idea how they would accomplish anything without raising the alarm, but the authorities were now becoming desperate for information.

There were just three weeks remaining before the diamonds were due to be transported to the British Museum, and there was always the possibility that they would be hijacked either on the way there, or when the exhibition was closing and the diamonds were to be collected. Those were the most vulnerable times, but even then, there would be such a heavy security presence that it would be a difficult nut to crack. There was also an urgent need to ascertain exactly what subversive activities Okorie had planned for the UCP to take up during the heist, if the diamonds were indeed the target. There were so many significant probabilities that required some sort of clue, and so it was essential that the group get answers as soon as possible.

The six operatives elected Murky as the main lead for the group, and they met the following day to discuss tactics. Murky ventured the opinion that the *Ardent Voyager* would be heavily guarded with an unknown number of heavies on board. Any attempt at a frontal onslaught was the last thing they should consider. Finally, Ben suggested a risky plan, but in reality it was the only chance they had to gain entry.

'I think the first thing we need to do is keep the *Voyager* under observation for a period of time to determine exactly what we are up against in terms of numbers. Once we are satisfied we know their strength and daily routines, we can contemplate how to board her and render the occupants ineffectual. One thing I thought about was using something like Agent 15 (BZ), but it would cause too many problems such as the need to wear a breathing apparatus. We also wouldn't want it to spread along the wharf and annoy the rest of the sailing community.'

Ben was an extremely likeable character: he was always jovial and never considered anything to be too big a problem to overcome. He had been great friends with George and Stuart, and whereas George was always the more reserved and quiet one of the group, Stuart and Ben were far more mischievous often egging each other on, which invariably got them into some misfortune. There was one subtle difference, though: Stuart would only want to fight his way out of a tight corner, but Ben would be straight in there with fists flailing around. Inevitably, it normally ended up with George, who got them out of trouble. It was only by chance that Ben wasn't the third member of the kidnap situation that took Stuart and George to Africa, because at the time he and his family were living in Washington D.C. while his father worked in the British embassy. His tour ended weeks before the boys were returned to England. Ben and George both had the spirit of adventure in them, and they'd decided to join the paratroopers at the same time. They had excelled in all the fields required and went on to enter the SAS. They were lucky that they remained together as part of a team of four, and they were taken under the wings of Jonah and Murky.

Once they listened to what Ben had to say, and after one or two questions, they felt there was a possible, albeit risky, way forward. One point that needed more clarification was how Ben thought they could ultimately board *Voyager*, incapacitate the occupants without them knowing, and get all the information they needed without leaving a trace.

'Ah! I see dissenters in the ranks. It doesn't matter what we do – it will be obvious that they have been rumbled with their cover completely blown. Of course, if Okorie is innocent of all we suspect, I imagine we will be hung out to dry, with our hierarchy denying all knowledge of us. We'd be looking at ten to twenty making mailbags for Her Majesty. The important thing is that we do get as much information as we can, because at the very least, it will disrupt their plans, considering the arrival of the diamonds are due so soon. It will take a good week or so of observation to determine when to strike, by which time delivery will almost be upon us.'

'Okay, Ben, but with regard to boarding her, what did you have in mind?'

Ben said he had a few ideas and said that he would give it some more thought while they set up a system of surveillance on the yacht and decided on which night to strike. It was generally agreed that it would need to be done in the darkest hours.

Once they had agreed how to keep the *Voyager* under surveillance, and who would take which shift, they reconnoitred the area. As it turned out, it wasn't going to be too difficult keeping watch because the ship was moored adjacent to the Mermaid Pub in Port Solent, and a watching brief could be kept without raising any suspicion.

Connor asked whether they might be barking up the wrong tree because if it *was* being used as a headquarters, he felt that they might have moored the *Voyager* somewhere a little more unobtrusive.

Ben had already considered this and said, 'The thing is – and I am assuming this – to have her moored in amongst regular seafarers would mask her real intent. And besides, this is really all we have to go on, as weak as it may seem.'

They decided that they would take it in turns to have a soft drink and make it last a couple of hours at a time, knowing they could claim reasonable sums back for refreshments. Since there were six of them, they decided that the best way forward would be to ensure that they didn't appear in the same pairs regularly, but alternate which person would be with whom.

It took two days to establish the number of people on board, six, and the occupants took it in turns to pop ashore to eat, two at a time. It also looked like there was some kind of pecking order in that the last two ashore appeared to be more privileged. They always stayed till closing time, availing themselves of the food, but they never appeared to drink any alcoholic beverages.

The team decided to continue watching for another two days to ensure that the pattern was being regularly repeated before making the final plan to board the *Voyager*. It appeared that the crew had not a care in the world; they had befriended most of the bar staff and one or two locals.

One evening, Murky decided to strike up a conversation with one of them just to see how receptive he would be to talking to someone he didn't know. As it turned out, he seemed friendly enough and readily accepted Murky's offer to buy him and his friend a drink. Murky steered the conversation to how disenchanted he was with living in this country, with little opportunity to better himself. That naturally led to questions being asked about what Murky actually did. Jed Engles, as he identified himself, had asked whether or not he was in the forces or police.

'I used to be in the infantry but got dishonourably discharged for hitting a superior officer. He was the biggest prat you could ever meet; apparently his daddy was a colonel with a string of honours after his name. He tried to shaft me by blaming me for one of his cock-ups. I now try to get work where I can as a minder, but some nights, I am outside night clubs as a bouncer.'

'That sounds a bit grim. What did they do to you for hitting the officer?'

'I got busted from corporal and sentenced to a hundred and twelve days in Colchester.'

'Colchester? What do they do there?'

'Colchester is where you become dehumanised with constant drilling, meagre rations, and being made to do things like polish your bucket every day to make it gleam after cleaning out all the crap and piss from the night before.'

In order to avoid any possible suspicion, Murky left it for one night but went in again the following evening, where he made his way to Jed and his colleague.

They talked about many things, and then Murky casually asked about their yacht. 'Is that your yacht? You must be fairly well off to afford the mooring fees here, let alone the cost of running such a beautiful vessel.'

'I wish. I am the skipper, and Harry here is like the first mate and navigator. Our boss is a wealthy West African gentleman called Afolabi Okorie, and he does a lot of business in London.'

Murky remained in their company until closing time, and he pretended to get more inebriated as the evening went on.

As time was called, Jed and Harry asked if Murky would be there the following day, but he said that he had a job as a bouncer for the evening to earn a few bob.

'Where will you be working? Far to go?'

'No, just Weatherspoon's. It's an easy one for me.' Murky pretended to stagger off as he bade them both a good night.

The group had been meeting every day to discuss events, and they felt it was fortuitous that the crew on *Voyager* were keeping to their routine. Once Ben felt they had seen enough, the group decided to meet some distance away to begin planning their assault. In three days, they would make their move. Ben set out his plan on how they could best achieve their goal.

CHAPTER 9

MURKY ENTERED THE bar, and as he had been doing on previous evenings, he ordered his drink and then made his way to Jed and Harry.

'Hi, there. Did you have a good shift as a bouncer the other night?' Jed asked.

Murky thought that it was a strange question, and he was naturally guarded when he asked what he meant.

'Well, we went to Weatherspoon's and didn't see you there!'

'Why?'

'We wanted to see how you handled unruly punters!'

Murky said, 'Do you know how many Weatherspoon's there are in the area? They looked at each other, appearing to be a little embarrassed. 'I have to say that I am a little annoyed that you wanted to check up on me. You know what? I think I'll just drink on my own tonight, thank you.'

He started to walk away, feeling that there would now need to be a quick change of plan, but Jed called him back.

'Jack,' Jed said, using Murky's fake name, 'I'm sorry. I didn't mean any harm. It's just that I am always a bit suspicious when a stranger starts up a conversation.'

'Why?'

'As you can imagine, there is a lot of expensive stuff on board!'

'And you think because I am scratching around for work, I'm going to jump aboard and nick a load of stuff? Nice!'

'Let me buy you a drink,' Jed offered.

Murky accepted his offer but said he would like an orange juice and lemonade with no ice. He was relieved that the plan his team had been hatching was still on track. It needed a lot of good luck for everything to fall into place, and then there was a chance of success. When Jed asked why no beer, Murky replied that he had an early start in the morning because he had a job to do.

Naturally, Jed wanted to know what it was, and Murky simply said that the owner of Hug's Jewellers' in Gosport had a delivery of a great deal of gold and silver items he wanted collecting, and he didn't want to take any chances.

This seemed to satisfy him, although Harry just looked at Murky and gave away no emotion at all. He was the quieter one of the two, but it didn't matter whether Murky was to be believed, because the team had planned to board the *Voyager* at closing time that night.

Murky kept up the lies, making the stories as interesting as possible and using some of his life's experiences to keep their attention. Finally, last orders were called, and Murky said he would like to buy the final round. Jed and Harry accepted. Just as Murky approached the bar, Ben walked to the bar behind Murky. This wouldn't arouse any suspicion because the two of them were never seen together. Murky reached into his pocket to get his wallet out, and as he opened it, he secreted two small sachets of flunitrazepam into his hand. Ben made sure that Jed's and Harry's vision was obscured from the bar as Murky slipped one sachet into each glass.

Hoping beyond hope that the two of them would completely finish their drinks, Murky took the glasses across to where they were sitting and went back to collect his own drink.

'Well, gentlemen, cheers. I doubt I will see you for quite a few days because once I've done this job for Hug's, I am going to London to look after someone's house. Although it's a crap job, it pays well.'

The barman shouted out it was closing time, and to Murky's relief, both men had completely emptied their glasses.

It didn't take long before Jed began slurring, saying he wasn't feeling very well. Harry looked worse for wear. Pretending to appear concerned, Murky went over to Jed, asking if he was all right, but by this time, he was barely able to string two words together.

He looked across at Ben, who came over. Between the two of them, they manhandled Jed and Harry out of the bar and into the fresh air.

Ben and Murky started to act as though they were drunk and sang loudly as they approached the *Voyager*. 'Ish thish your lickle boat, Jed and Harry Shwarry?' They were making a huge commotion as they tried to scramble aboard, dragging their so-called companions with them. This naturally alerted all those on board the *Voyager*, who scrambled out of the cabin and into the cockpit.

They were approached by a surly gentleman, who grabbed Jed and dragged him into the cockpit.

'You bloody fool, Skipper. You were supposed to stay sober!'

Ben made out to hug the man, but both were promptly told to leave the yacht. They pretended to playfully refuse, demanding that they be given another drink. 'Come on. The pub hash closed, and ush and our mates over there're shtill thirshty.

All the time this distraction was going on, out of sight of the crew, Jonah, George, Connor, and Brenden had sculled a dingy across and began boarding *Voyager* at the bows. It didn't take long to overwhelm the occupants, and soon all were trussed up like chickens. The problem was that there were only five of them.

'Where is the other crew member?'

The surly crewman spat in George's face. Jonah backhanded him, causing him to spin and fall to the floor. The man said, 'Who the bloody hell are you? This is a private yacht, and you have no right to be here. You have absolutely no idea who you are messing with!'

Jonah placed his face menacingly close to his ears and said who they were. He explained that if the man didn't answer his questions, he would soon find bits missing from his hand.

Again the man spat, and Jonah punched him again. Then he grabbed the man's fingers, curled them into his fist, and began to squeeze. He screamed in pain, but Jonah applied the pressure even more.

The others were rummaging around, looking for any evidence. Brenden opened a closet with a large safe inside.

George went to Jonah and put his arm on his shoulder. 'Leave him alone old, son. There is no way this will be hidden from Okorie, so it doesn't matter that the sixth crewman is missing. What we do want to know is the combination to the safe, and I feel your talents may be needed to find out what it is.'

Jonah carried on squeezing the fingers, and he menacingly demanded to know who had the combination. Finally, the pain was too much, and the man shouted that only Jed knew.

'We may have to wait quite a while until Jed here is more lucid, so we'll ask some questions. It's up to you how you want to go about it, because Jonah here really does hate hurting people, but when it is in the interest of our country, he has absolutely no compunction about what methods he has to employ. We are representing the British government, and we know a great deal about what you are planning, but you need to fill in the bits that are missing.'

'We really don't have the first clue what you are waffling on about.' This came from one of the men who had so far kept quiet.

Murky felt it was now or never and a bit risky, but he decided to mention what they had suspected Okorie was up to. 'You have one last chance before I unleash Jonah. We know about the diamond heist and the Urban Commandos. What we don't have are the dates!'

'Get stuffed!. We know nothing about that.' The look on his face, however, told a completely different story.

'Okay, Jonah, time to produce your little box of tricks.'

Jonah went across to the one who had just spoken and removed the tool bag from his jacket. After taking out the finger clippers, he began to roll over his victim.

The man began shouting and struggling, but to no avail. 'I know what those bloody things are! I'll kill you when I get loose!'

'Nice threat, but by the time you are loose, my friend, you will be devoid of most of your fingers. I may leave one of your thumbs so you can still wipe your backside. This is your last chance!'

'It's 55-24-63-00! That's the combination for the safe! Now for God's sake, put away those clippers!'

Connor went to the safe and opened it. There was a huge packet filled with documents, and he distributed the contents roughly in equal parts to his five comrades.

It was Ben who found the incriminating evidence, and when he enlightened the others, they looked at each other in horror. There was very little time to prevent a major catastrophe in London, because Okorie had installed a safeguard. There was a directive that any interference in his main goal would automatically invoke the mobilization of the Urban Commandos. It was a complex system of regular contacts being made at specific times within the network of his agents. There was also a system of passwords, and if contact hadn't been made within five minutes of the scheduled time, it would trigger notification to Okorie, who would then activate the Commandos. That scheduled time had expired forty-five minutes earlier. After looking through the rest of the papers, it was clear that the Commandos planned to riot throughout London, firebombing the whole city. It was not clear whether firearms were to be employed.

'We need to get hold of Major Bradley now. Secure this yacht and its crew, because we have all the incriminating evidence we need. It is beyond any reasonable doubt that the diamonds were Okorie's target.'

Major Bradley was awakened by the phone ringing, and once he had been briefed, he told Murky to hold the *Voyager* and wait for the police to secure it. The police arrived twenty minutes later while Murky was still on the phone.

'I will ring Emma Belchin and get an armed response team activated immediately.'

Murky told the major that it would be better if they used their special abilities in stealth to raid the house where the HQ was. Also, from the evidence gathered, the whole riot would be orchestrated and launched from a nearby warehouse.

'As soon as we have handed over to the police, which I think will be in the next few minutes, my team will be on the way to the house in E17. We anticipate our time of arrival to be about three hours. We have established that the warehouse is situated in the Blackwall Trading Estate. If you could have the armed team on standby, we will keep you informed, sir. The trouble is that although the warehouse seems to be the epicentre of the riots, we don't know whether there are any other cells that could still launch an effective attack. If we can neutralize the source, there is a good chance we can minimize any potential impact.'

The major was content to let the team try before mobilizing any other forces. That way if they were successful, it would prevent panic in the city, not to mention the potential loss of kudos for Great Britain.

They requested that Major Bradley contact the guard room of 12 Regiment Royal Artillery to allow the team to gain access to the vehicle park and armoury. There was a good chance they needed to be armed, and they collected weapons and a vehicle large enough to quickly transport all six of them to London. They left Port Solent in a convoy and reported to the guard room, where they availed themselves of all they needed. Then they set off towards their target.

On the way up, they began to make initial plans for how they would tackle the situation. Once satisfied, the subject of George's incarceration on *Voyager* was bought up.

George did say that it felt weird when he first boarded her, and nothing much had changed; it was still kept in pristine condition. 'The strangest feeling was walking past the cabin where Stuart and I slept. I remembered how frightened we were of Klaus and Jürgen. Even now, I still doubt I would be a match for either of them!'

CHAPTER 10

AFOLABI OKORIE HAD been extremely busy in the penthouse suite at the Radisson Hotel, Canary Wharf. He was entertaining a group of very wealthy foreign dignitaries who were in the market for weapons and associated munitions. The highlight of the night was to be the parade of young Eastern European girls who had been lured into Okorie's clutches with the promises of careers in modelling. In reality, he was auctioning them off to the highest bidder, and this was the part he loved the most. He had been doing this sort of business for many years, and invariably he would try some of his wares before any of his guests arrived. In particular, he loved the ones who resisted; as a cruel man, he would beat his victims into submission, which made him feel powerful. Of course, once in the penthouse and upon being made aware of the real purpose of their presence, the girls tried to fight to escape, and so they obviously needed to be subdued by the use of drugs.

Once the evening's business had been concluded, there was the odd guest who lingered longer, but eventually he managed to close the door as the last one vacated. Two girls had been chosen to wait in his bedroom, and he couldn't wait to have his way with them. After a very successful night's business, he made his way to his room.

His mobile phone had been in overdrive since midnight, but because he didn't want any interruptions, he had turned it off. He had never been this clumsy before, and it would cost him dearly. It wasn't until 2:46 in the morning, just as he was about to enjoy the delights of his two Polish victims, that he turned it back on.

Afolabi Okorie was born in Nkwanta, Ghana, of very poor parents. As the youngest of five, he was spoiled mostly by his mother, but his father also clearly favoured him above his older siblings. He was a big child, and so he took whatever he wanted; no one was big enough to stop him. It was of no concern to him that given what little there was of food, he would satiate his own hunger first, showing no concern for those who had to go without.

It is often said that no child is born wicked, but in Afolabi's case, he was born the very epitome of evil.

His brothers detested him for the way he was able to manipulate their parents, and they would often gang up on him when their parents were not present.

By the time he was thirteen, only one brother remained alive; the others had mysteriously met with tragic accidents that Afolabi had orchestrated, and he managed to appear totally innocent of their tragic demise.

At the age of nineteen, he had joined a local gang who terrorized surrounding communities. Within the year, he had disposed of their leader. The remainder of the gang were too frightened to challenge his leadership. As a brilliant tactician, he transformed the gang into an efficient crime organization, and by the age of twenty-five, he had accrued a personal fortune of several millions of Cedi, which equated to over one million pounds sterling. However, he made many enemies within the gang because of his greed. If anyone questioned him about their share of the money, he would beat the man to a pulp. Once the gang had served their purpose, he ditched them and moved on to bigger things.

When he did finally switch on his mobile, he went into a violent rage, causing the two girls to become whimpering messes. They tried to avoid his wrath, but he beat them both, leaving them bleeding and badly bruised.

He then calmed down and made contact with his right-hand man, telling him first to get someone into the suite to clear up the mess, and then to meet him at the warehouse. He arrived with his henchman at ten to three.

Murky and his team disembarked their vehicle ten minutes after Afolabi.

'Okay, that's the warehouse. Now we need to find a way in.' George suggested that it might be a good idea for Ben to scout around the back; they would wait to hear from him before making any move.

Ben was definitely up for that because out of the group of four, in all their deployments, he was the best one to scout ahead. 'Give me an hour, guys. I need to take a really good look around before we make a move. That way, we can hopefully minimise the need for violence. If I don't show by then, I think you will need to come looking for me!' He made his way across the road and disappeared into the darkness.

While they waited, they took note of all entrances and possible ways occupants might make a break for it. It was essential that whoever was in that warehouse had to be neutralized as soon as possible.

As the hour ticked by, George was becoming more concerned for his friend. An hour was the most time he would need because the warehouse was enormous, but even so, it was getting close to the time with no sign of Ben.

Eventually, George said that he had a gut feeling something was wrong, and they should move. They agreed and furtively moved towards the building.

Brenden forced an entrance through a side door, and the five of them entered carefully, fanning out to the left, right, and centre. It was extremely dark inside, and it took several minutes for their eyes to adjust.

Murky was in the centre and ushered both flanks forward, crouching as they went. They could hear voices somewhere in the depths of the building, but it was difficult to establish from which direction the noise was coming.

It was clear someone was being interrogated, and the voices became louder as they approached two wicket doors on the left and right sides of a huge wall.

All five drew their firearms, with Jonah taking the left door and Connor the right. They pushed open the doors and carefully entered the room. Moments later, there was an eruption of shouting and a cacophony of gunfire. Jonah fell to the floor as a bullet crashed into his kneecap, leaving him writhing in agony.

A split second later, Connor was thrown back with force, his forehead showing a crimson spot where a bullet had entered his head. As he spun from the force of impact, Murky could see that there was a huge hole in the back of his skull; he had been killed instantly.

Murky shouted through the door. 'Throw down your weapons! We have the building surrounded!' He then fired off two shots while George contacted Major Bradley to send back-up.

There was a great deal of shouting and a return of gunfire, but it was evident that whoever was there was making a break for it.

The three remaining team members decided that the only way to try to take control of the situation was to attack, and so they carefully opened the doors, looking for any cover inside the room. Once they had established what lay ahead, they remained low but charged in, firing their weapons. They were just in time to see whom they assumed to be Okorie being ushered out of the back, surrounded by his henchmen.

Quickly taking stock of the situation, they discharged their weapons and managed to down three of Okorie's bodyguards. They tried to give chase but two of the wounded men engaged them with small arms fire, pinning them down. From their cover, it didn't take long to neutralize them, but it was too late to reach Okorie.

Within twenty minutes, London's SWAT unit had arrived, leaving Murky, George, and Brenden to take stock of the situation.

Jonah was in a great deal of pain, and it was unlikely he would ever walk properly again, but thankfully he was still alive. Connor's body was covered up with a tarpaulin that was lying around. There was no sign of Ben.

Major Bradley arrived at the scene and went straight to George, who was tending to Jonah's wound.

Murky looked around the building and could hear a faint whimpering sound. He went to investigate, and it came from an adjoining room. As he entered, he almost vomited, and the shock of what sight there was before him was sickening.

Ben was trussed up naked, and there wasn't a square centimetre of flesh that hadn't been cut. There was blood everywhere, and even more sickening, they had gelded him. The blood poured from his body.

Murky went straight to his side, but Ben was barely able to talk. Murky put his ear nearer to his face, and he finally understood what it was Ben was saying.

'End it for me, Murky. Please, end it …' His voice trailed away, and he died in agony.

Knowing how close George was to his school friend, he looked for something to cover him with before he came looking for him. It was too late. George entered the side room, and although he looked at the mess that was once a human being, he didn't initially recognize him. It took a few moments for reality to register, and then it hit George like a sledgehammer. He quickly went to Ben and knelt beside him, cradling him in his arms.

He looked up at Murky, who indicated that Ben had died a few moments earlier. George's face was contorted with grief. He hugged his little friend and rocked him back and forth, and his tears were in free flow. He was unable to stop sobbing as a flood of small memories crept into his head of the times that he, Ben, and Stuart had had together when they were young boys.

Murky put his hand on George's shoulder to offer some comfort, and Major Bradley walked in. He too found it difficult to control his emotions, but he knew he had to try and mollify George. 'He will be buried with full military honours, my boy. You can count on that.'

Suddenly, George placed Ben's body back on the floor very gently. Disregarding the people around him, he marched straight in to the large area where two of Okorie's henchmen were having their wounds seen to. He made a beeline for one of them and ignored the shouts from Major Bradley. George grabbed him around the scruff off his neck. 'Who did that to my friend in there? Speak now, or I will slit your grubby little throat!'

The man looked up and could see murder in George's face. He was in a great deal of pain caused by the bullet wound in his chest, so he offered no resistance. 'It was Afolabi Okorie, I promise. I don't have any stomach for what he did.'

'Then why didn't you try to stop him? Why?'

Major Bradley put his arm around George's shoulder. 'Let him be, son. I believe him. What poor Ben went through is not the work any civilized person. Let's leave the clearing up to these good folks. Jonah is already on his way to hospital, but he will most likely need a walking stick from now on. Thank God, he will live to tell the tale. We lost two good men tonight. Connor's family will be informed later today, as will Ben's parents.'

'I would like to tell Ben's mum and dad. I won't tell them how, but I'll say that he was killed whilst preventing a terror attack on London.'

At this point, Emma Belchin entered the warehouse and went straight to where the major, Murky, and Brenden were trying to placate George.

'A good night's work, gentlemen. The team who took over from you on board the *Ardent Voyager* found a goldmine of information. There were in fact twenty cells in and around London. Only three became active, and they were neutralized within the hour. Whatever the delay was with Okorie mobilizing his Commandos, it was fortuitous. There have been several raids and hundreds of arrests, and London can rest easy after having kept its credibility.'

George asked, 'Has Okorie been arrested?

'I'm afraid we don't know where he is, but I'm pretty sure with his network of support, he will have fled the country before too long. It is most likely he will try to get back to Ghana, where he can lie low for a while. We have only hurt him slightly – we haven't destroyed him. He is still an extremely wealthy man and has a great deal of influence in some circles around the world.'

Murky then turned to George and said now that the threat to him and his family had been effectively lifted, it was time to bring Jayne back from hiding. 'Poor girl has been away with the Erkinshaws for five weeks. I bet she has been worrying herself sick over what you've been up to. You need her to help you through the trauma. It is bad enough for us, mate, because we loved Ben as well, and we also know how far you go back.'

George agreed and asked if he could leave now. 'Since this seems to be over, I no longer wish to serve, and therefore I will be requesting my release!'

'You and Jonah have been free to leave any time you like; you were only called back to deal with this situation. Thank you. You have both served your country with distinction.'

CHAPTER 11

GEORGE WENT TO Ben's parents' house two days later because he was exhausted and needed to rest. He also had to consider how he was going to break the news.

He was dreading knocking on the door, knowing that initially the family would be pleased to see him and invite him in like old times.

He needed a hug, and the person capable of giving him that warmth and love was on her way back from France and due to arrive that evening. Although he was looking forward to being reunited with the love of his life, it didn't do much to lift the way he felt inside.

He was beginning to regret volunteering to do it, but deep inside, he knew it was his duty to speak with the family of one of his oldest and dearest friends.

George parked his car outside Ben's house and waited for a few moments to let the dreadful churning in his stomach settle down. After taking a deep breath, he went to the front door.

It was Ben's mother who answered it and as soon as she saw who it was, her face lit up with a huge smile. 'Come in, George. It is so nice to see you! Ben isn't here at the moment. In fact, he is due to come home in a couple of weeks for some leave. His dad and I can't wait to see him because he has been away for almost a year.'

George swallowed hard and asked if they could all sit down, because he needed to talk to them.

Her face changed to one of confusion; she could see that something was clearly bothering him, and so she ushered him into the lounge, where her husband was sitting.

'Hello, George. Nice to see you again, young man. It has been a while.'

'Albert, Cathy, I don't know where to start, but I am so very sorry to have to tell you that Ben won't be coming home. I'm afraid he was killed the other night while preventing a terrorist attack in London two days ago.'

There was a stunned silence, and it was clear that Ben's parents were struggling to comprehend what they had just heard.

'How did he die? He didn't suffer, did he? Oh, my poor little boy!'

Cathy broke down uncontrollably. George found it difficult to breathe because his throat had constricted with the effort it took not to cry himself. He had no intention of telling them that Ben had been horribly tortured and mutilated. Instead, he said that he had died bravely saving not just his life but the lives of those in the group.

'Was this to do with the failed riots in London the other day?'

George nodded, and he noticed tears streaming down Albert's face.

It was all too much for George, and he began choking back his own grief. When Ben's mother walked across to him to hug him, he could hold it back no longer.

The situation deteriorated further when Ben's younger brother and sister entered the room. They had heard the commotion from their bedrooms. 'What's the matter, Mum and Dad?'

Cathy composed herself, stood, and walked towards her children. 'I'm so sorry, guys!'

She tried to take a deep breath, but as she did, she was hiccoughing as she tried to catch her breath.

'Mum, you're scaring us. Please tell us what has happened!'

'Ben has died, darling. He was killed two days ago while on duty in London.'

They all sat down. Albert and Cathy were just able to control their emotions now, but Ben's siblings were beside themselves.

'I'm so sorry to have to bring such terrible news to you all. It is one of the saddest times of my life. We have been mates since the age of five, and I have lost one of my best friends.'

Albert put a hand on his shoulder to comfort him. 'It's a bad business, son. Ben was doing something he loved to do, especially having the opportunity to serve with you. Does Stuart know yet?'

George said that he didn't, but he planned to visit him in the next week or so. With that, he excused himself and apologised again for bringing such sad news. After a tearful farewell, he left. It left a bad feeling inside, and he began to seethe at the injustice of it all.

'That was no way to die, trussed up like a Sunday joint and tortured.'

George knew why he had been mutilated: Ben wouldn't talk. Despite the pain and being helpless and naked, he would have never endangered his comrades, and so he was cut dozens of times with a knife. Then there was the final humiliation of that filthy pig Okorie, manhandling Ben's private parts and then cutting them off.

George had to stop the car. Up until now, he had been devoid of any feelings other than sadness, but after having seen Ben's family, the sadness he felt was replaced by a silent rage.

He said a little prayer and then vowed to himself that he would redress Ben's torture and humiliation by visiting something ten times worse upon Okorie. He had made up his mind: he would avenge his friend no matter what it took. Okorie was going to suffer.

CHAPTER 12

JAYNE WAS NATURALLY very excited to hear that the danger was now over and that she and George could hopefully get back together. She was desperate to get back into the routine that they had enjoyed before this nightmare started.

The Erkinshaws were sad to see Jayne leave; they had grown to love her as a daughter. They took her to the airport and hugged her tightly. For her part, Jayne had grown to love them too because they were such a lovely couple.

'You and George are welcome to come and stay any time you like, my darling. It has been such a pleasure to have some young company to talk to in the evenings.'

Jayne hugged them once more and turned to go into the departures lounge, waving wildly as she disappeared through the barriers.

Like George when he was flown back to the UK earlier that month, arrangements had been made to clear her through immigration because they had both illegally entered France five weeks before.

The plane took off on time, and it was only a short flight finally before they landed at Southampton Airport. She got her baggage and made her way to meet George in the lounge. When she clapped eyes on him, she dropped her bags and ran straight into his arms.

He swept her off her feet and hugged her as if she was about to disappear. He was so pleased to see her because he needed her gentle touch and to hear her voice again.

Jayne told him, 'Thank God this nightmare is over, darling. And thank God you are safe.'

He didn't say anything but kept hugging her, and then he started to break down.

Jayne released her grip and gently pushed George's shoulders away, looking him in the eye. 'George, what is it?'

At first he couldn't speak, and then finally he managed to find his voice. 'Ben was killed while we were stopping an attack on London.'

'I don't understand. What did that have to do with someone trying to kill you?'

'It's a long story, poppet, but it is all connected. I will explain as much as I can later.'

There was something in George's face and expression that Jayne didn't like. 'It *is* over … Isn't it, George?'

He picked up her bag, put his arm around her, and said, 'Not now, poppet. Let's go home and get reacquainted. My name is George. What's your name?'

She smiled and moved closer to his body, and they walked off happily together. If she knew what was going on inside George's head, she would have been horrified.

Once they arrived home, all the evidence of what had happened the night that caused their flight from the UK had been removed, apart from a small stain on the carpet.

Jayne shivered involuntarily as she remembered defending herself and the way in which she had killed her adversary.

'Don't worry, sweet. We will change the carpet and have the house redecorated. That way we will remove most of the memories.'

'It's only been a few weeks, and yet it feels like a lifetime ago when we were last standing here. I don't think I can relax enough to be able to sleep here tonight, darling; it doesn't feel right. Can we go to an hotel for a while, just until the house has been redone?'

George acknowledged what she said, and he suggested that they contact Stuart and ask if they could stay there for a few days. 'That way, we can get the decorators in to transform the house.'

When Stuart heard George's voice, he erupted with joy, saying that they would get a spare room ready for that evening.

'Are you coming tonight, old friend? Katy will be over the moon to see you!'

George thanked him but declined the offer. 'There is someone I need to see this evening, but would it be okay if we came over tomorrow?'

'We will look forward to seeing you both in the morning. We are not intending to go on tour for a couple of months, so please stay as long as you want. We have so much to tell you both.'

They booked into the Marriot Hotel in Portchester. Once settled, George said he had to quickly pop into 12 Regiment Royal Artillery, and he would be back soon. 'It appears that when we signed for our weapons, I had omitted to tick certain boxes. I know – bureaucracy gone mad!'

He hated lying to Jayne, but he was driven by a burning hatred of Okorie, and he wanted speak to Danny Knight to seek his advice.

It only took twenty minutes to get to his house, and George hoped beyond hope that Danny was in. He was relieved when he saw a shadow approach the door, and he was greeted by Dawn, who at first didn't recognise him.

'Oh, my goodness! George! Come on in. Danny is in the lounge. Would you like something to drink?'

George declined but went through to where Danny was sitting, and he took the seat that was offered.

'Well, what a lovely surprise! But judging by your face, you haven't come here to chew the fat and pass the time of day with the usual small chat, have you? In fact, as I remember, you and your wife were wanted for questioning about three murders. I hope you're not going to tell me you are still on the run!'

George apologised if he appeared rude, but he acknowledged the fact that it wasn't a social visit.

Danny smiled and said, 'If it isn't you, then what trouble has Stuart got himself into now?'

'It's not Stuart, Danny. We both had another very close friend, Ben, whom you never met. His father was sent to Washington D.C. on an accompanied tour for two years. He left England some time before we met you, and he came back just before we arrived in the UK, after our little adventure. Ben and I joined the army at the same time and were lucky enough to serve together. He was mine and Stuart's best friend.'

'What makes me feel that I'm not going to like what I'm about to hear?' Danny was aware that there had been an attempt on George's life because at the time, while grasping at straws, it was thought that it was a case of mistaken identity.

'The whole thing is connected. It's a long story, but as it turns out, the events that took Stuart and me to Africa is linked to what this has been all about.'

At first Danny wasn't able to comprehend what was being said, but George explained briefly what had happened since they had last met. He openly wept when he got to the part where he described the horrors of Ben's last moments.

'So it was you and your group who were behind those little skirmishes in London the other day! I have to say that I wasn't familiar with the name Afalobi Okorie and the *Ardent Voyager* until now, but I can see where you are coming from.'

'I can't help but blame myself. He was always good at seeing the lie of the land, so I suggested he go to look around the back. That was the last time I saw him alive.

He died moments before I walked into the room where that bastard Okorie had tortured him.'

'I'm confused, son. Why have you come to me? I am no longer active as a soldier, and Dawn and I are thinking of retiring in a couple of years. It's an age thing!'

'Sorry Danny. I am not trying to recruit you. This is my fight, and I intend to find that piece of filth and send him to hell – but not before he has suffered. The reason I have come is to ask whether you have Hendrik's address in South Africa. I would like to ask his advice because I want to go to Ghana to find Okorie.'

'Let me get this straight. You intend to go to Ghana – not a small place by any means – to find Okorie and kill him? I'll bet you don't even have his address, do you?'

'That's why I would like some advice from Hendrik; he knows Africa better than anybody. I haven't got a clue yet what my plan is, but I've got all the time in the world. Stuart is seeing me all right for money, and when this is over, I will go back to teaching – if I survive.'

'Let me guess: your young wife has given her blessing … not!'

'You are the only person who knows what I plan to do, and I know I will get grief from Jayne, but it is something I have to do. I can't rest until I have avenged Ben. There was no dignity in his passing, and no animal, let alone a human being, should ever be allowed to die that way.'

'As far as Hendrik is concerned, you can ask him yourself; he is coming over for a visit in two weeks with his wife. Give us a ring, and we'll arrange for you to come to dinner. Please ask that crazy friend Stuart and his wife to come too. I know Dawn would be over the moon to see him again!'

'We would love to come to dinner but as far as speaking to Hendrik about Okorie is concerned; I would rather do that privately.'

Dawn had diplomatically left the room when George had started to talk to Danny, but she re-entered and insisted that he at least have a drink. He refused, saying that he had to get back to Jayne, who would by now be wondering where he had got to.

He arrived at the hotel just after eight in the evening. Jayne had showered and was showing a shapely leg through her dressing gown. This did get George's immediate attention, and he asked whether or not going down to dinner could wait for about half an hour. She smiled, and her tenderness and warmth radiated through him. It allowed him to forget the horrors of the past few days, and they finally went to eat.

George felt slightly better the following morning when he awoke, and he looked forward to seeing Stuart. They hurriedly packed after breakfast and made their way to the outskirts of Oxford, arriving there at lunchtime.

As soon as Katy heard their car pull in to their drive, she was beside herself with excitement and ran out to hug George. 'How are you, my horrible older brother? Oh, my gosh, you look really well. It is so nice to see you.' She kept hold of him for several minutes and then turned her attention to Jayne, whom she had never met before. 'And you must be the long-suffering woman who has kindly offered to put up with old grisly here, we were both so sorry we couldn't get home for your wedding but we had a contract to fulfil in the States!'

Jayne smiled and said that she knew what she meant. 'He can be a grisly pain sometimes, but he'll do!'

Just then, there was a loud whoop from the house. Stuart came running out at speed, grabbing George while trying to give him a bear hug and spin him around. He lost his balance, and both men ended up rolling in the drive, laughing hysterically.

'You always were a big, awkward sod, but you're looking good – ugly, but good! It is so wonderful to see you. Come on. And by the way, you're far too good for him, Jayne.'

She smiled warmly and gave Stuart a big hug as they walked in together.

'All we need now is for Ben to come and make it a complete reunion. Any idea where he is these days?'

George's demeanour changed in an instant, and he said that he needed to talk to Stuart alone.

Katy said, 'Let's have some lunch, guys. You two can talk while Jayne and I prepare it, being the good little women that we are.'

Stuart sensed that there was something very wrong; it would have been difficult not to have, given the way George's mood had changed. 'What's up, old friend? You look really troubled.'

'Ben will never be coming home again, Stoopot. He died horribly the other night at the hands of Okorie.'

'Okorie? Why does that name mean something to me?'

George told Stuart the whole story about how the attempt on his life had led to the raid in London several weeks later. 'It seems that fate has dealt a terrible hand to us, and the way that Ben met his end was without pride or dignity. I need to ask a really big favour.'

Stuart found it difficult to take it all in, and he kept asking the same questions in slightly different ways. In the end, as it dawned on him what was being said, he cried. 'I don't understand, why did he do that to Ben? It doesn't bear thinking. You said you had a favour to ask. What can I do?'

George explained that he intended to hunt down Okorie and kill him. 'I was going to do the same to him, but that would make me as bad. Besides, I know I couldn't do that to another human being. He will suffer, though. I will use mind games on him before I finally finish him off. The thing is, I have obviously been paid by the government for my service of late, but it won't stretch to mounting an assault on that sack of shit.'

'George, as I said before, you can have as much as you need. But are you sure you want to do this? It will be very dangerous, and I really couldn't afford to lose another good friend. What does Jayne think about it?'

'Oh? What does Jayne think about what?' She and Katy had entered the room carrying trays of food.

It was no good trying to fob either of the girls off. He couched his words carefully, leaving out some points, but he explained what he had to do.

Katy was beside herself because although Ben had already left for America before her brother and Stuart had got into trouble, she used to tease him horribly when she was younger. The topic took the edge off the reunion and the special lunch that had been prepared.

They stayed for just over a week, by which time their house had been transformed, and they were prepared to move back. George said, 'Don't forget, we have been invited to Danny and Dawn Knight's for dinner next week, so we'll see you both again very soon.'

There was a very tearful farewell as they left, with Stuart and Katy begging George to think again, but on seeing he was determined, they made him promise to be careful and not take any silly risks. It was a futile effort because deep down they knew he would stop at nothing to get revenge. Neither Stuart nor Katy had seen George like this before.

Once home, George and Jayne set about making their house habitable. It did look completely different, with the new décor and carpet. It was a relief because Jayne had toyed with the idea of moving, but on seeing it through different eyes, she felt more at ease.

CHAPTER 13

ON THE DAY that they were due to have dinner with Danny and Dawn, Stuart and Katy drove down to George and Jayne's to spend the afternoon with them. After a riotous welcome, they were invited in. As they walked through the lounge, Stuart began to giggle. When asked what he had found so funny, he explained that the last time he had trodden these floorboards, he was being frogmarched in with a bucket of soapy water and a sponge waiting for him in the kitchen.

They sat and enjoyed a light lunch, and Katy asked whether Jayne had managed to change George's mind about seeking revenge. The look on Jayne's face spoke volumes. It left all present knowing that it was a taboo subject.

Katy then decided to lighten the mood with her news. 'Stuart and I are happy to announce that we are expecting a baby, and it is due in six months. George, you are going to be an uncle!' Everyone was delighted, and that became the topic of conversation for the rest of the day.

On the way to dinner, Stuart was naturally curious about how well Dawn had aged over the years.

George said, 'Crikey, mate. She is only in her late-forties. And yes, to satisfy your obsession, she is still a very beautiful woman!'

This earned Stuart a whack from Katy, who felt the conversation to be totally inappropriate.

They arrived at Danny and Dawn's at seven and were ushered in. A slightly older-looking Hendrik grasped both men in a bear hug.

'It is so good to see you both again after all these years.' He then realised that he had not presented them to his wife, whom he introduced as Monica.

Once they had familiarised themselves with each other, they sat and chatted for a while. Before they went in for dinner, Hendrik asked if he could have a quiet chat with George.

'It's okay, Hendrik. Jayne and Katy both know what I intend, so any advice you can give would be most welcome.'

'Danny has given me a rough brief of what you want to do. I imagine Okorie has fled back to his main powerhouse in Ghana. That being the case, apart from the fact I haven't been engaged in subversive activities for years, Ghana is well beyond any areas of influence that I might have had. The only thing I can suggest is that you find where in Ghana his main influence is and start there. It shouldn't be too difficult because before you and your group exposed him for what he is, he was the darling of most European governments. You could glean a great deal from the Internet.'

George accepted the advice, and with the matter closed, they all went in to eat.

Jayne had volunteered to drive, so all four men drank copiously, which created an atmosphere of hilarity. As one would expect, it was Stuart who was the main source of the laughter.

As the evening drew to a close, there was an emotional parting with promises of meeting up again once George's quest had hopefully concluded successfully.

On the way back home, Katy asked when George planned to leave.

'I have applied for a visa saying I wanted to explore their country, and I only planned on staying for about two months. I'm hoping to leave sometime next week.'

'So soon? I wish you would reconsider, George!'

Jayne said that she didn't want to think about it, because every time she did, it filled her with great trepidation.

Stuart and Katy left the following morning amongst floods of tears and wishes of luck for the future. As good as his word, Stuart had transferred a huge amount of money into George's account, and so George was all set to kit himself out.

Unbeknownst to George, Murky had rung Jayne to find out what was happening, and when she explained that the expedition was imminent, he asked if she could let him know when he intended to leave, with flight times and dates. When she asked why, he said that he would try to see him off and give some last-minute advice.

'Please don't tell him, Jayne. I want to make it a surprise because I may have some information that might be useful to him.'

The visa arrived the next day, and so the decision was made to leave on the following Wednesday.

When the day arrived, Jayne said she would rather say goodbye from home and not at the airport, because it was upsetting enough as it was.

'I'm a very lucky man to have you, Jayne. Not many wives would tolerate this. Thank you so much for being brave and understanding. I promise that I won't take any unnecessary risks, and if I think that what I plan could put my life in danger, I will abort the mission.' He kissed her passionately and then was gone.

All the way to the airport, he thought about different ways he could find Okorie. Also, he wanted desperately to make him suffer mentally before finally killing him. Naturally, he was filled with doubt, but then he dismissed it immediately as he forced himself to remember the bloody mess that was once his best friend. The journey to the airport was a complete blur because he was lost in thought.

He was about to check in when there was a tap on his shoulder. On turning around, he was surprised to see it was Murky.

'What on earth are you doing here?' George asked.

'Ah! Now, that didn't work out how I thought it would. You see, I thought you were going to say how pleased you were that I am coming with you.'

'I don't understand. How did you manage to get time off?'

'You didn't think I was going to let you loose in Africa on your own, did you? When I spoke to the old man, he felt that the leave I had taken to help you out proved to be the downfall of the Urban Commandos and the exposure of Okorie. As a result, I have been given leave to enjoy exploring Ghana. As far as he and Emma Belchin are concerned, if I am caught, I will be cashiered out of the army with a possible spell in prison on my return to UK, with no parole for at least a week.'

'You have no idea how pleased I am to see you, old friend. I really appreciate the offer, but it is one hell of a risk. If we do get caught inside Ghana, we are unlikely to see home again.'

'We will have to be careful then, won't we? Anyway, I know where he is. We have been using contacts we have in the area, and it appears that Okorie was wounded when we burst in that night. He is in St Joseph's Hospital.'

'You are a bloody genius, mate! You have just made the whole thing a lot easier, but we still need formulate a plan because that bastard needs to suffer a bit before I kill him.'

'Before *we* kill him! Don't forget that Ben was a good friend to me too. I know you both go back a long way, but we shared a lot of danger and experiences together as well.'

George agreed, saying that he had given some thought to what to do and that they would go through the plan together on the way to Kotoka Airport.

The flight was uneventful, and once they landed, they hired a car and headed north along the N2 motorway towards Nkwanta. At Kotoka, they asked advice regarding hotels in Nkwanta, and they made reservations at the Park View, which was not far from St Joseph's.

Once at the Park View, they booked in to their individual rooms and were relieved to see that there were many other Westerners staying there. They would therefore be less conspicuous.

It was decided that they would put their plan into practice the following day. In order to throw off any suspicion of the reason why they were there, they asked the concierge where the best remote places were to sightsee the wildlife. They explained that they intended to start exploring in the morning.

In the morning, they donned backpacks and drove off, making their way to a card shop some distance away. They bought a set of cards. After that, they began to put their plan into practice, hoping and praying that it would go smoothly. They spent the day reconnoitring beyond the outskirts of Nkwanta and venturing into the rural areas. Once satisfied, they returned to their hotel.

The following morning, they drove to a spot a short distance away from St Joseph's and stopped a young child who was on a bike. 'Do you speak any English?'

The boy smiled and nodded.

They handed him a card with a few Cedi, asking if he would take it to the hospital. He looked in his hand, keeping it open and shaking his head. They put a few more coins in, and he shoved it in his pocket. They told him that if he came back here in the afternoon, he would be given another card and more money. He smiled broadly and left.

The envelope was addressed to Afalobi Okorie, and it was taken direct to his room, where he was being tended by his henchmen.

Okorie opened the envelope and was suddenly thrown into a terrible rage. Inside the card was a crude sketch of a skull with the words, 'Get dead soon!'

Immediately, one of his men ran down to reception, demanding to know who'd delivered it, but the boy had long since gone.

Later that afternoon, the boy reappeared at the same spot. He took the second card, and before he left, he was told to be there at ten the following morning, where he would be asked to do the same again. The lad couldn't believe his luck.

This time, the card still had the same crude skull drawn on it, but the words said, 'Not long now, and you will be a dead man – and it won't be quick.'

It was a little childish in some ways, but George wanted Okorie to become unsettled in his own backyard.

Again, one of Okorie's men raced to the reception, but the boy had already left.

The following morning, as promised, the boy showed up again and took the card, but this time he was told to wait for a reply. They would wait there for him to come back with a man from the hospital. They also told him to come back at the same time the following morning.

There was a scream from Okorie's room when he opened the latest envelope, because it depicted a man who had been gelded and was bleeding to death. The drawing was crude, but it left him in no doubt what the sketch meant.

This time, the youngster was waiting for the inevitable henchman who, when he met the boy, was about to rough him up but then thought better of it.

Once he had established that the boy knew where the sender of the cards would be, he got the directions and sent him on his way. They boy was disappointed that there was no money for him, but he would get more the following day when he met the two men again.

Meanwhile, George and Murky had changed their positions and waited a little farther up the road, concealing themselves from view.

Eventually, a car arrived with three men inside who appeared frustrated that there was nobody there. They were about to depart when George appeared from behind the wall and then ran back. The men gave chase. On reaching the corner, the first man was met with a huge blow to the head from Murky's makeshift truncheon. The second man stumbled into the first one, meeting the same fate. The third man was totally confused and he fell to Murky's blow.

The men were trussed up like Christmas turkeys and thrust into their car. Then George drove the hired car, and Murky drove the thugs car to a prearranged spot that they had recced the previous day. It was secluded, and it seemed nobody had been in the vicinity for some time. Murky was to stay overnight with the men, who kept making threats, but they were bound so tight that they were barely able to move.

At ten in the morning, George handed the last envelope to the young boy, giving him a large wad of cash and offering to drive him to the hospital himself. The lad smiled and climbed in the car with him. At the hospital, the envelope was handed in to the receptionist, who called over a porter to deliver it. As the porter left, George followed him.

The porter nervously knocked on the door, and he could hear an angry voice asking who it was. He entered, offered the envelope, and quickly left. Two minutes later, there was a shout from inside.

The card had read, 'Today's the day you die. Your three companions lie at the bottom of a river as you read this, and you are next.'

There then followed a silence. As far as George could establish, Okorie seemed to be in the room on his own. George thought it was now or never.

He furtively entered the room, and Okorie's face was one of fear and confusion.

'Mr Okorie, my name is Jenkins, and I work for MI6 in London. We have had credible intelligence that your life is in immediate danger. I have been sent here by Julien Alger, who is a government minister.'

'I know Mr Algar. How did he find out about this?'

'Mr Okorie, we don't have time for this now. There are some very nasty people on their way here as we speak. I managed to follow two of them yesterday, and they had somehow set up a trap. I believe three of your men were killed by them. I was very nearly seen and was lucky to escape with my life. You mean a great deal to our government, and we have to get you away now. I will explain on our way to the British embassy. I know it will be a long drive, but I need to secrete you away from here as soon as possible. Can you walk?'

Okorie nodded affirmatively and hurriedly dressed as George ushered him out of the door.

They took the stairs and in order to minimise the chance of him being recognised. George told him to put a large handkerchief over his face and pretend to blow his nose.

'We can trust no one, Mr Okorie. There is only me, with no back-up. Your government has refused help for some reason; apparently, they are blaming you for a rift between Ghana and Britain because of a problem in London some time ago. Our prime minister has been at pains to reassure your government, but there is still tension.'

Once out of St Joseph's, he got Okorie into the car and drove off casually, creating the illusion that all was well. He drove to the outskirts and on to where Murky was waiting with the other three men.

It wasn't long before Okorie became suspicious and started demanding to know where they were going. 'This isn't the way to the British embassy! I demand to know where we are going! You have no right, and you really don't want to mess with me. I could have you killed at the snap of my fingers!'

George looked at him and smiled a sickly smile. Despite Okorie's tough words, he was clearly frightened. He began to struggle and tried to swerve the car off the road, but George was a strong man and kept control of it.

Then without warning, George struck Okorie across the temple with his elbow. Okorie slumped forward. George hoped he hadn't killed him yet; that would come a little later. Okorie had to be aware that he was about to die, because that would add to the suffering.

George rendezvoused with Murky by mid-afternoon, and they put phase two of the plan into operation.

The three men were clearly the worse for wear, having spent a cold and very uncomfortable night with no food or water. Murky produced six bottles of whiskey, and one by one, he forced a bottle into each mouth, making them drink every drop. By the time he had finished, Okorie and the three henchmen were so drunk that they couldn't string two words together. It was almost comical to watch. The men were then untied, and all four were placed in the car's seats. It was a most difficult operation because they were all dead weights and tended to lollop everywhere.

Once they were all positioned satisfactorily, the remaining two bottles of whiskey were emptied all over the occupants and the interior of the car, and once the empty bottles had been thrown in and a cigar thrust into Okorie's mouth, Murky set a match to his clothes. He began to scream as the fire took hold, and it spread very quickly inside the car and then on to his companions.

They slammed the door shut and waited for it to take hold.

Both men positioned themselves on either side of the car as attempts were made to get out. Each time a door opened, the two kicked it shut.

Finally, the car was really ablaze, and Murky and George got into their vehicle and drove away as they saw the death throes of its inhabitants. Neither felt any pleasure at what they had just done, but at least the world was now rid of a very unsavoury man.

'Are we done here, old son? Murky asked.

'Ben has been avenged. Every time I think of the horrors I have just witnessed at our hands, I will remember little Ben's mutilated body. Yes, old friend, we are done. Thank you. It would have been a different story had you not helped. I may never have returned home in one piece.'

They took a huge detour, and as luck would have it, they saw no one else until they drove back into the outskirts of Nkwanta. There would be no way that the events unfolding in a quiet, secluded spot of Ghana could ever be associated with the two of them.

In order not to raise suspicion, they stayed for a few more days, pretending to take in all the sights. They finally made their way back to the UK ten days later.

The relief was almost tangible from those who were aware of what had happened. They were pleased that on the news, the authorities in Ghana had reported the deaths of Okorie and his three henchmen, saying it was the result of a drunken orgy. It was most unlikely that the authorities really believed that, but it was expedient to them because Okorie had become a bit of an embarrassment.

Once back home, George hugged Jayne and said that they could get back to having a normal life.

'Thank God it's over. It has been a terrible nightmare,' Jayne said.

They hugged some more when George said, 'Takeaway for supper, and copious amounts of alcohol?'

'Now that sounds like a plan. You're buying!'

Author's Note

Upon reading the first book in this series, a very good friend of mine, suggested that I might make its sequel a little less farfetched. My apologies Ant, but I have added quite a bit of pepper and salt in this one as well.

It is doubtful, for example, that retired Special Forces agents would ever be returned to active service as described here. Neither am I aware of such a tool that would remove fingers; they may exist, but I have never come across any.

It is appreciated that there may be a few inaccuracies in the story, but it has been written purely to entertain and to offer the reader a modicum of escapism for a short while.

As with my previous novel, any similarity to any persons living or dead is purely coincidental and not intentional.

About the Author

Charles Kramer was born in 1947 and joined the British army at the age of fifteen. He became an engineer and was attached to the 16/5, the Queen's Royal Lancers, until 1971. He left the army to work for the MoD. He began writing in the nineties, but owing to his computer crashing, he lost several thousands of words. It wasn't until twenty years later that he again put pen to paper. This is his fourth book and second novel. He has also written an autobiography and a children's book (the beginning of a series of adventures about a bear called Douglas). He is currently in the process of writing a second children's story.

The two novels are related, and a third is in the process of being written, with completion expected in the autumn of 2017.

Lightning Source UK Ltd.
Milton Keynes UK
UKOW02n1325250816

281502UK00002B/19/P